BABY TO A SCHEDULE

BY MAREE MANDERS

CHAPTER 1

*T*he day you have dreamt about your whole life and been planning for the past year since your engagement has finally arrived.

You are standing at the edge of the park on the foreshore of the beach, you look to your right and the love of your life, Chad Williams, is standing there next to you, you both met in your final years of high school and instantly fell in love and have been together for the past 5 years. You can't help but take in his strong angular facial lines, freshly shaven face, and his black hair shining in the sunlight. Chad looks over to you, gives you a wink and a cheeky smile.

You both turn your attention to the marriage celebrant in front of you. The time has come for your vows. The celebrant turns her attention to you, "Angela, are you ready for your vows?" You nod and smile at her. "Fantastic" she says, "Now turn to face Chad and the recite the vows that you have written". You pass your bouquet to your Maid of Honour, your best friend, Hannah, turn to face Chad and take his hands in yours and despite being in the presence of the celebrant, wedding party and all your close friends and family, you only focus on Chad, and feel as if you are the only two people there in that moment.

As you hold Chad's hands and stare directly into his piercing blue eyes, you begin your vows.

"My darling Chad, I have loved you from the first moment I saw you, I love your smile and sense of humour. You are everything to me, you are my world, and I can't imagine travelling the path of life with anyone other than you. I look forward to being in your arms every day for the rest of my life. I can't wait to see where our lives take us, but I know every day will be wonderful with you by my side as we share what is yet to come."

Chad looks at you with a loving smile and tears begin to form in his eyes. He gently squeezes your hands as he begins his vows to you. "My darling Angela, you are the love of my life, you have made me who I am today, your support never waivers. You fill my life with such love and happiness and can always make me smile, I look forward to sharing what may come with you and promise to make you feel special and loved every day of our lives".

You push back tears as you smile back at Chad.

"That was beautiful" the celebrant says, "Now we will exchange the rings".

As you place the ring on Chad's finger you recite "Chad, please accept this ring as a token of my everlasting love for you", Chad nods smiling. It is now time for Chad to place the ring on your finger, "Angela, please accept this ring as a token of my everlasting love for you." You nod to Chad smiling.

Turning back to face the celebrant, she now begins to finalise the ceremony. "We have all witnessed Chad and Angela expressing their vows to each other, watched them exchange rings. It is now my pleasure to proclaim them as husband and wife, Chad we all invite you to kiss your new wife".

You both turn to each other, Chad lifts your veil, he cups your face in his hands, looking deep in your eyes, he leans down and kisses you passionately. You wrap your arms around him and reciprocate the kiss with equal passion. Your guests erupt with cheers and clapping of hands. You finally part, turn to face your guests, smiling you join hands together and raise them high in the air in a fist pump. The clapping and cheering continue as you walk hand in hand down the aisle, getting ready to greet your guests as newlyweds.

The time comes during the reception for your first dance as husband and wife. As the music starts you wrap your arms around Chad and slowly move to the music staring into each other's eyes.

The reception draws to a close, you farewell your guests and prepare to leave for your honeymoon suite at your reception venue, for your first night together as husband and wife.

You reach the door of your suite, as you open the door, Chad lifts you up in his arms and carries you through the doorway. The room is stunning, the bed has red rose petals scattered on the white duvet and pillows, there is a bucket of champagne chilling in the corner and a tray of chocolate coated strawberries on the nightstand. Chad reaches for the bottle of champagne and slowly pours you each a glass, you reach down a take a strawberry in your hands and gently feed it to Chad, he does the same for you. You each take a sip of your champagne staring at each other. "Wow, what a day" claims Chad as he takes you in his strong arms and pulls you close to him. You look into his eyes and respond, "It was perfect, I am so happy". Chad nods in response and plants a kiss on your lips, you deepen the kiss. After a few moments, Chad pulls away, and smiles at you, "I think

I need to get you out of this amazing dress" he gently reaches to your back and begins to unzip your dress exposing your back. You begin to untie his tie and unbutton his shirt. Shortly after you are both standing there together in your underwear. Chad passionately kisses your neck, sending a sensation of pleasure through your body. You pull Chad over to the bed and playfully push him back, you climb on the bed straddling him and passionately kiss his lips, neck, and chest. You sense him becoming hard in his underwear as your hand reaches down, you release him, grab his penis in your hand and gently stroke it, feeling it harden even more in your hand. Chad, gently groans and then flips you on to the bed, moving his hands down your body from your neck, down your chest over your breasts, down your abdomen to between your thighs. He pulls your underwear off and places his hands between your legs, you moan in response and gently rock your hips closer to him. "Oh, my Angela, I love you so much",

"I love you too Chad," you respond almost breathless. Chad now moves over top of you, and you feel him at your entrance, "I want you now Chad" you exclaim, and he responds, you feel him penetrate and you both rock your hips together in unison. You both come at the same time and then lay together breathing deeply. You turn to face each other and smile and kiss each other passionately.

As you both lay in each other's arms, the events of the day catch up with you and you both close your eyes and drift off to sleep.

CHAPTER 2

*T*he next morning, you awake to the gorgeous warm sunshine filling the honeymoon suite and the sounds of birds cheerily chirping outside. You are still encapsulated in Chad's strong arms. As he lays still sleeping, you think about your plans now that you and Chad are finally married. You and Chad have made no secret of your dream to start a family immediately, so much so, that as soon as you became engaged, you began to plan for the best time for conception, luckily your cycle has always been regular, so as strange as it may seem to some, you devised a spreadsheet to track your monthly cycle. You relied on this spreadsheet when determining your wedding date. You wanted to make sure that your wedding date would coincide with the best time in your cycle to conceive. As you lay next to Chad, you place your hand on your stomach and think, "Could we have made a baby last night? Oh, I hope so". As your mind begins to dream about the thought of falling pregnant immediately, Chad wakens and pulls you in tight to him. "Good morning, my darling wife, how did you sleep?" You turn to face him, smiling, "I slept perfectly my dear husband" and you kiss him.

You turn to look at the clock and realise that you both need to get up quickly and begin to get ready for your trip to the airport to begin your honeymoon.

You both arrive at the airport with just enough time to check in and board your plane which will take you to Hawaii for a 7-day island getaway. As you settle in to your seats, Chad puts his arm around you and holds your hand with his other hand, He whispers to you " I can't wait to arrive and relax on the beach, it has been a busy last few weeks finalising all the plans for the wedding, it is going to be so great to just sit and do nothing, don't you think sweetheart?". You respond, "Absolutely, can't wait". You pull him close for a passionate kiss and then snuggle into him and prepare for take-off.

Several hours later, your plane descends into Hawaii and you both feel excitement build as you prepare for your time on this beautiful island. Shortly after you arrive at your resort and check in. The honeymoon suite has been reserved for you and when you open the door to the suite, it is beautiful. A large king size bed fills the room, and again has rose petals scattered on it. There is a beautiful bouquet of flowers on the desk and a fully stocked mini bar. The ensuite has an oversized spa bath, which you can't wait to use later. Chad moves to the sliding door, opens it and steps out to the balcony outside, excitedly he calls to you, "Sweetheart, come and look at the view, it is awesome". You join him on the balcony and look at the view, it overlooks the resort pool, and further out, you can see the shoreline and beautiful crystal blue ocean. "Wow, this is gorgeous, isn't it?", Chad smiles and nods and returns his eyes to the view, all the while holding you in his arms. After standing together soaking in the views and lovely ocean breeze, you turn to Chad, pull him in for a passionate kiss. As you pull away briefly you look into his eyes and say, "What say we test out this bed?", you playfully pull him back into the room, moving over to the bed and you both end up rolling on the bed. "Absolutely" Chad responds as he reaches to unbutton your top and places his hand inside your top rubbing your breasts. You place your hand on the back of his neck and pull him in for another passionate kiss, wrapping your arms around him, pulling him in tight to you. Shortly you are both naked, you feel his penis harden at your entrance you both moan with excitement. He penetrates you and thrusts with force, you feel the pleasure fulfill your whole body and you continue to rock your hips close to his in unison. Shortly after you both explode with excitement and hold each other and slowly try to regain your breath. You lay together, gently caressing each other's naked bodies.

After a while, you try but are unable to hold back your stomach from rumbling. Chad questions you, "Are you hungry? Do you think we should go and get something to eat?", You nod in response, get up, freshen up and dress for your evening meal.

The resort restaurant is fully stocked with an incredible buffet of local seafood, roast meats, and salads. After selecting from the buffet, you find an intimate table off to the side with a view out to the ocean and enjoy your meal.

After dinner, you both decide to take a walk along the beach, paddling in the shallow water. The sun starts to lower in the sky and you both sit on the beach watching the sun set in the distance. As the last of the sun disappears on the horizon, you head back to the resort in the moonlight and retreat for evening.

The next morning you both awake to the sounds of the waves breaking on the shore, today the plan is just to relax on the beach and let the stress of the final wedding planning from the last few weeks fade away.

The next few days of your honeymoon, involve relaxing on the beach, swimming in the resort pool and exploring the island in general.

The last day of your honeymoon has arrived, you both pack a picnic lunch and decide to explore the beach again, finding a secluded area of the coastline, you set out your picnic blanket and enjoy your picnic feast.

You both realise that you have been enjoying this peaceful area completely alone for the past two hours, not another sole has found this area. Chad looks at you with a cheeky smile, he grabs you and pulls you close to him and envelops you in a deep passionate embrace and kiss, you respond by deepening the kiss. Before you know it, you are both naked and sharing another passionate lovemaking session on the edge of the beach, the tide begins to change and water is soon lapping around your bodies, you don't mind, you are lost in each other and continue to bring sexual pleasure to each other. You lay next to each other in the shallow warm water now surrounding you. You turn to Chad, and say, "what a fantastic week, this has been, wouldn't it be fantastic if we have made our dream come true here on this beautiful island and made our baby?", Chad pulls you in tight and responds " How great would that be, I can't wait to have a baby with you, that would be the last perfect piece of our puzzle, making us complete" You nod in agreement and return to laying in Chad's arms.

After a little while, with still no one else around, you decide to dress and return to your suite to prepare for your flight the next day where you both will be returning to your normal lives.

CHAPTER 3

*I*t has been two weeks since your amazing wedding and your unforgettable honeymoon in Hawaii, it seems like a distant memory now as you both return to your usual routines. Chad is a Lieutenant at a very busy fire house, his job is demanding both physically and mentally as he deals with the experiences of his role, fighting fires, caring for the public and his own team in times of stress and panic. You also have a somewhat demanding job; you are the team leader of the finance department for a global marketing firm. Recently management have been discussing the possibility of opening a new branch in New Zealand, so leading up to your honeymoon, and since returning you have been working with management to plan the acquisition, both from a monetary and resource view.

As you prepare for the day of work ahead, you remember your baby plan, and open your cycle spreadsheet on your computer. You notice that now is the time when your period is due, and time now to take a pregnancy test to see if your dream of becoming pregnant on your honeymoon has come true. Chad is already on his shift at the firehouse, so you decide now is the time to take the test. You open and prepare the test. Your phone alarm is set for 3 minutes, and you nervously wait, styling your hair and applying makeup ready for the day. Finally, the alarm rings, your stomach begins to flip with nervousness and anticipation. You slowly grab the test and pull it close to you and at that moment, your heart sinks, it is negative. You fight tears away as you continue to prepare for the day, giving yourself a pep talk as you go, "Oh well, it didn't happen this time, things were quite stressful with the wedding and finishing up things at work before the honeymoon, it was probably stress, just relax and maybe next month".

By the time you arrive at work, you have pulled yourself together are ready to settle in for the day. As you are waiting for your computer to boot up, your boss Greta appears in the doorway of your office. "Good morning, Angela, how are you today?", You reply with a smile, "Good thanks and you?".

Greta responds, "Good thanks, can I see you in my office immediately please" and turns away and heads back to her office up the corridor. You stand up, knots begin to fill your stomach, you think to yourself, "Oh no, what is going on now,".

As you enter Greta's office, you notice Rick, the owner and CEO, sitting at the desk, perusing a file of papers.   "Good morning, Angela, please take a seat" and gestures for you to sit on the seat in front of the desk. As you sit down you gaze at both Rick and Greta, trying to see if you can read anything from their faces to let you know what you are in for, but their faces give nothing away. Rick begins, "Angela, thanks for joining us today, by the way, I haven't had a chance to see you since your recent wedding and honeymoon, congratulations", he finishes with a smile. The flips in your stomach, settle to small hops now. "Thank you, Rick, the wedding and honeymoon was wonderful, just as Chad and I had planned".

"Excellent" replies Rick, "Now Greta and I have asked you to come in here today, as we have a very important matter, we need to discuss with you. As you know, before your leave, we were heavily involved in planning our new operations in Auckland, New Zealand, well I am pleased to advise that the plans are finalised, and we can begin the set-up process immediately".

"That is great" you reply, excited that your hard work over the past few months has finally come to fruition.

"I am glad that you agree Angela," Rick replies, "We are now ready to staff the new office in Auckland and we would like you to head the setup of the Finance/Accounts and Marketing teams. We will need you to travel to Auckland, oversee the recruitment and training process for the finance and marketing teams".

"Oh wow" you respond, your mind is racing. "How long would I be required?"

"Well, we foresee at least two to the three months" Greta responds.

"Oh, I see" you reply, your mind still thinking to yourself, What about Chad? and your baby plans?

Seeing the puzzled look on your face, Rick chimes in, "Angela, we have watched you closely over your time here. We are so impressed with your work ethic; you have grown so much during your time here. We strongly appreciate your deep passion for your tasks, your ability to take on whatever task is put before you. You are methodical and we strongly appreciate the leadership and mentorship you have shown to the new starters that have come through our doors. It is for this reason that we feel you are the only choice to build the new finance and marketing teams in our new office".

You are humbled by the praise, and feel your cheeks begin to become flushed. Finally, you can respond "Rick, Greta, thank you so much for your kind words, it is wonderful to be appreciated for my efforts, I truly enjoy what I do".

"That's great to hear" responds Rick, "Now for the finer details of this new venture, As mentioned, we would require you to travel to Auckland for a minimum of two to three months, we will find appropriate accommodation for you, it is up to you of course if you would prefer a hotel, or apartment or house rental. We will provide you with a company car for the duration. We will also increase your salary in recognition of your new role as Training Manager, would an increase of $15,000 per year be acceptable?"

'Oh wow, that is amazing, but before I say yes, obviously I need to discuss this with Chad, Can I think about it and get back to you?"

"Oh, Ok, of course certainly, we understand" replies Greta, however, you sense an air of confusion in Greta's voice. "Unfortunately, as the plans to open the new office are in full swing now, we will need an answer by the end of the week, and we would need you to fly out at the end of next week".

You do a mental calculation in your head, today is Wednesday, that only gives me two days to decide, "Chad has just started a 24-hour shift, I will not see him until tomorrow night".

"Ok, Angela, please let us know as soon as you can on Friday, we would love to have you on board for this venture" says Rick as he stands picking up his paperwork and heads for the door and leaves.

Greta sensing your trepidation remarks "Angela, I understand you have just had your wedding, but Rick and I truly believe you are the best person for this role, and as we said, we only envisage it being for a period of three months at the most, we have already put feelers out for new staff applications for the new office, please think about this, it will be a wonderful opportunity, maybe Chad could travel with you, I know Rick would agree to that"

Smiling, you thank Greta and return to your office to try to settle in for the day's work. You decide to send a message to your best friend Hannah hoping she can help you to decide.

"Hey Hannah, how are you going today, Are you busy tonight? I need your advice on something that has just happened at work, will fill you in on all the details tonight".

Hannah is engaged to Trevor, one of Chad's fire station team, so you know that she won't have plans with Trevor tonight.   Shortly after your phone beeps, it is Hannah, "Hi there, yes, I am free, let's say we meet at Giuseppe's pizza at say 6.30pm, very intrigued to know what is going on, enjoy your day lovely"

The rest of the day passes by in a blur, you have such a big decision to make, that is all you can think about for the day.

As you enter Giuseppe's you notice Hannah sitting at the table by the window, it is not overly busy tonight, Hannah looks up, sees you and jumps up, as you reach the table she pulls you in for her traditional bear hug, squeezing you tightly, she says "Hey lovely, so good to see you, what's happening? I have been on tenterhooks all day".

"I need a drink first" you respond, you both order cheeky mocktails and she stares at you as if trying to read your face. As you take a sip of your mocktail, you begin to unload the events of the day, you begin with the devastation of finding out you were not pregnant this morning.

Hannah reaches for your hand and gives it a squeeze, " Oh love, I am sorry, I know how much you and Chad were hoping for a honeymoon baby, it was a pretty stressful time leading up to the wedding, what with all the work stuff you had going on as well, with the big expansion plan, Try not to worry, it will happen for you and Chad very soon I can feel it" She gives you a reassuring smile.

You then begin to tell her about the meeting with Greta and Rick and their offer for you to head up the building of the finance and marketing teams in the Auckland office. Hannah's face erupts with a huge smile and her eyes are wide, "Oh my god, that is fantastic love, you have worked so hard, it is great you finally have been recognised and rewarded". Her face turns to concern, "Why are you not jumping off the walls Angela, this is fantastic news?"

You reply, " I am excited Hannah, but I am not sure what to do" Hannah continues to look at you quizzingly, you continue "Yes, I know it is a great opportunity, and I am very honoured, but Chad and I have just gotten married, and you know our plan to start a family immediately, How can I do that, when I am in another country for a minimum of two to three months? It is not part of my schedule Hannah, what do I do?" your voice quivering.

Hannah gets up, pulls you into another bear hug, "Oh lovely, I know having a baby is so important for you, but this is such a great opportunity, have you spoken to Chad?"

Still in the hug, you wipe tears from your face and respond, "No not yet, I am waiting until he finishes his shift tomorrow, and I will discuss it with him tomorrow night over dinner".

Hannah pulls away, helps wipe the tears from your face and sits back down in her seat. "Chad will be so happy for you, he knows how hard you have been working at this firm, he will want you to take this opportunity, If I know him, and I think I do, he will be jumping off the walls so proud of you. I know it messes with your baby schedule, but it won't be for ever, and it is only three months you say, that is not that long, if you are asking me, I say hell yeah go for it, this is a great opportunity".

Nodding you smile at Hannah, "Ok, you're right, Chad will be happy for me, and he will want this for me, maybe he can spend some time in Auckland with me, that would be awesome".

"Excellent, that's settled, talk to Chad tomorrow and kick that promotions arse" Hannah smiles, "Now what the heck are we going to eat?"

As you and Hannah share a meal, dessert, and hours of chatter about anything and everything, you notice the wait staff begin to clean and pack up for the evening, "Oh crap Hannah, we are the only ones left in here, I think they want to close up".

"You're right Angela, I think we better settle the bill and let them close up and go home".

As you return to your cars, you give each other another big hug, Hannah smiles and says" You got this girl, I am so proud of you". You smile at Hannah, thank her for the great chat and make the trip home.

As you lay in bed alone, while Chad is at work, your mind wanders, "I think I can do this new job, it is only for three months, Chad can come over, it will be awesome" smiling you eventually fall asleep.

CHAPTER 4

You are suddenly awoken by your 6am alarm. As you pull yourself from your bed, you notice the all too familiar pain in your stomach, your period is about to start, "Crap, well that definitely confirms the test from yesterday, not pregnant".

You busily prepare for the work day ahead and head off to work, you know that Chad's shift at the firehouse will be ending soon, Quite often you are like ships passing in the night, Chad returning home as you are heading off, you can't help but look at the oncoming traffic to see if you can recognise his car, unfortunately you don't see his car heading home.

You arrive at work and think ahead to your dinner with Chad tonight where you will discuss the promotion offer and the failed pregnancy test.

Conversation scenarios run rampant in your head, how I am going to start this conversation, you think to yourself, heck what will we even have for a meal?

You try to push these thoughts out of your mind and concentrate on the budget you need to prepare by the end of tomorrow for your team, however the thoughts keeping sneaking back. If you are truly honest to yourself, you want this new role, but you can't help but feel selfish, this is not part of our plan, our baby schedule.

Finally, the clock shows 5.00pm and you can clock off for the day and head home to Chad.

As you open the front door, the familiar fragrance of your favourite beef casserole greets you. Chad has started preparing dinner already. As you enter the kitchen, Chad looks up from chopping the vegetables, "Hey sweetheart, welcome home, how was your day?" He pulls you in close for a passionate kiss and hug. You reciprocate and then respond, "Yeah, work was fine, I am pretty tired, thanks sweetheart for preparing dinner".

"No worries sweetie, just relax, dinner won't be too long".

You head to the bedroom, change into your old sweatpants, freshen up a bit and return to the kitchen.

As you wait for dinner to finish, you chat to Chad, about his shift, luckily it was uneventful for him.

"Sweetheart, take a seat, I will serve dinner and bring it over to you" Chad gestures for you to head over to the dining table while he begins to plate up the wonderful meal. As you head towards the table, you stomach begins to flip flop, knowing that you must talk to him about the failed pregnancy test and the promotion offer from Rick and Greta.

Chad comes over to the table, places your dinner in front of you, takes his seat across from you, as he does, he looks at you with concern. "Sweetheart, are you okay? you look upset?"

You look back at him, thinking how I begin, "No I am okay, just tired, let's eat this fantastic meal!", unconvinced, Chad looks at you for what seems like minutes, then begins to eat his meal. You know this is not over, Chad will question you again after dinner.

You sit in silence eating your dinner, Chad still looking at you frequently as if trying to work out what might be happening.

As you finish dinner and clean up the kitchen, Chad pulls you in close, leads you to the couch "Sweetheart, I have known you long enough, I know when something is bugging you, please tell me what is wrong".

Sitting on the couch, your hand in Chad's you look at him searching for a way to start your conversation.

"You're right, there is something, actually two somethings I need to talk to you about" you pull your eyes away from Chad.

"Okay" responds Chad, he pulls your hand closer squeezing it tighter, "You can tell me anything sweetheart, go on", you can sense the anticipation in his body rise.

"Ok, Chad, I will tell you, ok, to start with, yesterday morning, I checked the baby schedule spreadsheet, and it was time when I could do a pregnancy test".

"Ok" responds Chad, you sense a mixture of excitement, and anticipation in his voice, which makes it harder to continue.

"Well, I took the test" fighting back tears you continue, "I am sorry sweetheart, it was negative, I am not pregnant".

"Oh" says Chad, pulling you close to him, kissing the top of your head, "Sweetheart, don't be upset, it is ok, it was only our first month trying, we can't expect it to happen straight away, think of all the fun we can have as we keep trying". You try to laugh, but only tears flow, "he moves you back, wipes the tears from your face, "Don't cry sweetheart it is alright" You move closer to him, resting your head on his chest, he continues to rub your back consoling you. "You had me really worried, is that was what was worrying you? it is ok sweetie, it will happen."

As you lay in his arms your mind drifts to the other problem you need to talk to Chad about.

"Oh Chad, that is not all I have to tell you",

"Oh, that's right you mentioned that there was another something you needed to tell me about".

Pulling away from Chad, As Chad looks at you intently, you start to tell him about the meeting yesterday with Rick and Greta, "Yesterday, Rick and Greta called me into Greta's office, to talk about the new office in Auckland they are ready to open the new office at the end of next week".

"Wow that has happened fast" interjects Chad,

"Yes, it is, they need someone to recruit and train new personnel for the Auckland office and they have offered me the role".

Chad's face lights up, "That is great sweetheart, what a great opportunity".

"Yes, it is, but there is a problem, they want me to travel to Auckland, to interview and train the new staff".

You notice Chad's face change slightly, "Oh I see, how long will you need to be away?"

"They are saying at least two maybe three months at this stage".

"What did you say to them?"

"I said I needed to discuss it with you obviously".

Chad takes a deep breath, "What do you want to do? Do you want the role?"

"I think I do, it would be a great opportunity, and there is a pay rise involved, which would be awesome, but I am worried about leaving you, and abandoning our baby schedule".

"When do they need an answer?"

"Tomorrow, as they would need me to leave at the end of next week, if we decide I should take it".

Chad's body stiffens, "Wow, that is definitely fast, I am not going to lie, I am taken aback by this, we have just gotten married, three months sounds like both a long time and a short time all at the same time, yes, it certainly stuffs up our baby schedule, I thought that this was our dream, but on the other hand, I know how hard you have worked for this, I don't want you to go obviously, but I won't stand in your way. If that is what you really want, I will support you, you know that".

"Greta says that you can come and stay with me any time you want".

"I can't do that sweetie, it is not easy for me to take furlough at a moment's notice, there is a lot of planning that needs to happen, my spot has to be covered on shift, and we have just had time off for the wedding and honeymoon".

You sense his jaw tighten as he speaks, which adds to your confusion. "So, what will you tell Rick and Greta tomorrow?"

Standing up, you turn to Chad, "I want to say yes, but only if you are sure, you are ok with it".

Chad stands up, grabs your hands, pulls them up and kisses them, "As I said, it will be hard to be away from you for three months, but I refuse to let you miss out on this opportunity, you have worked so hard, you deserve this promotion, I just wish you could stay here in Brisbane and not have to leave for Auckland, bugger, if you want this, then go for it,"

You throw your arms around Chad's neck, pulling him close and kissing him passionately.

"Thank you, sweetheart, thank you for your support, I love you so much".

CHAPTER 5

As you arrive at work, you make your way to Greta's office to let her, and Rick know that you have decided to take the promotion. As you approach Greta's doorway, Greta looks up and notices you and smiles, "Good morning, Angela, how are you today?"

"Really good thanks, and you?"

"Great thanks Angela, how can I help you?"

"Greta, I have been able to speak to Chad about the promotion offer and have reached a decision".

"Ok, great, come in, close the door, take a seat and let's discuss this".

You enter her office, close the door behind you, and then make your way to the couch in Greta's office. Greta takes a seat next to you, eyes fixed on you, "Ok Angela, let's talk, how did the conversation with Chad go last night?"

"Well, I explained the opportunity to Chad, and the need for me to be in Auckland for at least two to three months. Naturally, Chad was concerned about the need to leave him for that length of time, especially considering we have only just gotten married, however, being the wonderful man he is, and he is supportive of my career, and fully supports my need to do this. So, Greta, I would like to accept the role please."

A smile fills Greta's face, "Oh that is wonderful Angela, as Rick and I discussed on Wednesday, we believe you have great people skills and are an excellent trainer, and we know you will be the best person for this role." She claps her hands together. "Great, I will let Rick now immediately, and we will start to make the necessary arrangements. Now, would you like us to source a house or an apartment? Or would you prefer a hotel room?"

"Oh, I haven't really thought that far ahead", you pause for a moment. "I think a house would be a bit excessive for just me, an apartment will be fine,".

"Good choice, leave it with me, I will get right on to it, now just to let you know, we have organised for Derrick to join you in the new office, he will be setting up the IT side of things, so you won't be alone".

"Ok, that's good",

Derrick oversees IT in the office, and you get along well with him, so you think that will be fun.

"Ok Angela, I will get started on all the plans, and I will get back to you later today. Oh, this is going to be great, Congratulations Angela, oh, by the way, is Chad going with you next week?"

"Oh, unfortunately not, he is not able to get any time off, we have just had time for the wedding and honeymoon".

"Oh, I understand, that's a shame though", with that Greta stands up, you join her, she shakes your hand smiling infectiously.

As you leave Greta's office, you feel a sense of relief as well as excitement for the next chapter that is about to start.

Later that afternoon, Greta swings by your office, "Hi Angela, I have your air ticket here, we have you leaving next Friday morning at 11.am. We have found a lovely furnished apartment for you close by the new office; we have also arranged for a car for you to use. The keys will be at the apartment building reception. All the details are in this compendium for you. I have also included a short list of potential applicants for the various roles we need filled perhaps you could peruse these this afternoon and begin to set up interviews for your first week".

"Great, thanks Greta, I will look through these now" as you take the compendium from Greta. You begin to sense how real this is becoming.

As promised you peruse the short-listed applicants, and choose your own shortlist, you decide to make calls to them first thing on Monday morning to set up interviews for the following week. You pack up and head home, taking the compendium with you to show Chad.

The next week flies by, you have been able to successfully organise a full week of interviews for your first week in Auckland. On Tuesday evening, you were able to schedule a farewell dinner with your parents. Your parents are important role models for you, they have been together for more than 30 years, married for 25 years. Their love for each other has always been an inspiration to you, you feel privileged to have found Chad, your soulmate and replicate the wonderful connection that your parents have been able to share for all those years. The relationship you have with your Mum is so special, you both are extremely close, like kindred spirits, and more like best friends than mother and daughter, you have always had the dream of having a similar relationship with your own daughter one day.

Before you know it, it is Friday and you and Chad are on the way to the airport to catch your flight to New Zealand. As you arrive at the airport and check in, your stomach begins to turn in knots, with both excitement about the new opportunity, but at the same time, you are dreading the knowledge that you must be separated from the love of your life for close to three months. Chad places his arm around your shoulders as you walk to the gate to board your plane. As you reach the gate the realisation that you will be leaving Chad, takes over, and tears begin to well in your eyes. As you stop and turn to Chad, you notice tears forming in his eyes also. "Well sweetheart, this is it, I have to head through the door here to meet my plane."

Chad's arms tighten around you, and pulls you in close to his chest, you feel his heart beating so fast. You look up into his eyes and plant a kiss on his lips. Chad reciprocates deepening the kiss. After what seems like minutes, you finally part and move towards the door.

"I love you Angela, I will miss you so much, you will rock this sweetheart, I love you so much".

"Thank you, sweetheart, I love you and will miss you so much, we will facetime every night, it will go fast, and I will be back as soon as I can.", you respond,

Chad nods, "yes we will facetime every night, good luck sweetheart,"

You both hug and kiss again, you finally pull away and back your way through the airport door, blowing kisses as you go.

As you enter the plane and find your seat, you wipe the tears from your eyes, and tell yourself that "this is a great opportunity, and you will be fine". As you take your seat and wait for the plane to take off, you try to think ahead to when you arrive in Auckland and imagine what the apartment will be like.

After managing to rest your eyes for a little while, you wake up to flight stewards preparing the cabin for the descent into Auckland. As you descend, you see the city of Auckland below with the farmland backing onto the sprawling city. As you land, excitement begins to fill your body and you begin to smile. As you disembark from the plane and head through the walkway to enter the airport, you notice a man in a blue suit standing in front of you holding a placard with your name on it. "Oh, Greta and Rick have organised a driver for me, that's cool" You walk up to the driver, smiling you say "Hi, my name is Angela Williams".

"Hello, Madam, how are you? my name is Paul; I will be your driver today".

"Hi Paul, I am great, how are you?"

Paul responds, "I am good Madam, let's get your bags and I will take you to your apartment", He turns, and you follow him to the baggage claim and collect your luggage.

Paul takes your luggage and leads you out of the airport towards his car. You feel like royalty as you are chauffer driven to your apartment, you look out the window and take in as much of the city as you can. You take in the magnificent city skyline. A smile beams across your face and before you know it you have arrived at your apartment building, the Maui Heights, which will be your temporary home over the next two to three months. Paul gathers your bags, and escorts you through the majestic entry doors towards the reception, it is there he bids you farewell, wishing you all the best for your time here. You thank him for his expert assistance, placing a generous tip in his hand, and turn to face the receptionist and check in to your new apartment.

The receptionist, a young fair headed lady, greets you with a beaming smile. "Mrs Williams, pleasure to meet you, my name is Sandy, and I will be more than happy to help you with anything you need".

"Thank you, Sandy, please call me Angela, I am so excited to finally arrive".

With that, Sandy finishes your check in process, explains the features of the building, hands you the key to your luxury suite and the keys to the company car that is parked in the basement, for your own personal use, during your stay.

A baggage porter meets you and assists you to your apartment suite.

As you enter suite 602 you are met with an exquisite level of luxury, the room is tastefully decorated with neutral tones, and has floor to ceiling windows overlooking the city centre. The views are magnificent, you thank your porter, giving him a tip for his service and then you are alone to take in your new surroundings. As you pan around the room, your eyes find the most amazing bouquet of flowers on the table, there is a note peeking out from the amazing buds of roses. You open the note and read it out loud to yourself,

"My darling Angela, I miss you already, I know you will be a great success, I am so proud of you always, your forever loving Chad, XXX". You clutch the note to your chest and smile widely. For the next half hour, you unpack and familiarise yourself with your new lodgings.

CHAPTER 6

Before you realise it, the time has just gone past 6.00pm and you realise that you are getting hungry, you head downstairs to the restaurant in the building next door.

As you wait for the elevator, you sense a familiar presence next to you, you turn to see Derrick, standing next to you.

"Hey Derrick, when did you arrive here?"

"Hi Angela, I arrived earlier this afternoon, it is a beautiful apartment building, isn't it?"

"It certainly is, have you seen the views out the window, absolutely amazing?". As you wait for the elevator to reach your floor, you turn to Derrick, "I am just heading out for dinner, I thought I would try the little Italian restaurant next door, Sandy at reception, said it was magnificent".

"Hey great minds think alike, I was just heading there myself" responds Derrick with a smile, "Care to join me? he adds.

"Why not, sounds like a great idea" just then the elevator arrives, and you both enter and ride down to the lobby.

As you exit the building, the early autumn night air is starting to descend, and there is an obvious chill in the air, you begin to shiver slightly as you walk hurriedly to the restaurant. Derrick notices, "Are you cold Angela, do you want my jacket?" He begins to take off his jacket for you.

"No No, Derrick, I will be fine, it is not far, in fact we are almost there, thanks anyway, I will just have to get used to the cool air here."

As you enter the restaurant, a bubbly waiter greets you, "Good Evening Sir, Madam, a table for two?"

"Yes, that would be lovely," answers Derrick. The waiter gestures you both follow him as he leads you to a cute little table in the corner by a roaring fire. Derrick pulls out the chair for you, as you both take your seats, the waiter continues, "My name is Mario, and welcome to Alessandro's this evening, can I interest you in a drink while you peruse the menus?". You both agree to a glass of white wine and begin to look at the menu.

As Mario returns with your drinks, you both place your orders for dinner. "Fine choices" Mario responds, dinner will be served shortly,

As Mario leaves, you turn to Derrick "So, how do you feel about being here for the next two months or so?"

Derrick, like yourself, has recently been married.

"Yeah, it is going to be hard, I miss Bree already, it has been the first time we have been apart since we married last year".

"I know it's hard, as you know Chad and I have only been married for less than a month, it was really hard to leave him, but I couldn't pass up this opportunity".

"Gee, yes, you have only just gotten married, haven't you? You are still like on your honeymoon basically".

"Yes, thankfully, Chad is so supportive, and encouraged me to do this, we will talk every day, as long as he is not on shift of course"

"Yes, Bree and I will be chatting daily too, she is planning on come up for a week or two, if she can get time off her busy job, so that will be something to look forward to, Is Chad coming to visit at all?"

"No unfortunately, Chad can't get time off, we just had the time off for the wedding and honeymoon. Being a firefighter lieutenant, it is hard to take time off, so we will just have to rely on facetime calls etc".

"Oh wow, that will be hard", With that your meals arrive, and you enjoy your meals and chat about life and work for the next hour or so.

"Well, that was really lovely, Hope you don't mind, but I think I will head back to my suite and call Chad".

"Glad, I bumped into you tonight, it was great to see a familiar face on my first day here, no problems at all, I want to call Bree anyway".

With that you pay for your meals and walk back to your apartment building.

The air outside is even colder outside, you feel yourself begin to shiver again. Even though it is only a few hundred meters to the building, you feel you will freeze before you reach the door. Derrick looks at you, "here come here" he reaches his arm around you and pulls you in close under his warm jacket. The warmth of his body is so inviting, but you are torn as you feel that you shouldn't be this close to another man other than Chad, you know it is simply Derrick being gentlemanly, but you pull away, and respond, "Thanks Derrick, but I will be fine, besides we are nearly there".

Derrick looks at you apologetically, "Oh sorry Angela, didn't mean to make you uncomfortable,"

"No Derrick, you didn't, sorry, I am fine".

Just then you arrive back at the apartment building, ride the elevator in silence back up to your floor. As you step out of the elevator, your arms brush past each other.

"Well Derrick, thanks for a lovely dinner, it was so great having someone to share my first night here with".

"Yes Angela, it was a lovely night, are you heading to the office on Monday, I will see you there?"

"Yes, I have a number of interviews lined up on Monday, so I will see you there", with that you both say goodnight and return to your apartments.

As you enter your apartment, you settle on the couch and pull out your phone to call Chad.

"Hi sweetheart, just checking in, how are you going back home without me?"

"Hi Darling, I am fine, it is very quiet here, I just got back from dinner with Hannah and Trevor, what have you been up to? How is your apartment?"

"Glad, that Hannah and Trev are looking after you, the apartment is gorgeous, the views of the city are amazing, I will send you some photos soon. I met Derrick, he arrived today as well, and we had dinner together".

"Oh Ok, that is good then, what will you get up to tomorrow?"

"The weather is pretty cool, but I think I might take a walk and check out the area and do a bit of sightseeing, and then prepare for the full day of interviews I have lined up on Monday".

"Oh, that sounds good, dress warmly, send me some pics when you can, that will be great, I am missing you so much, wish I could be there with you,"

"Me too,"

"Oh well sweetheart, I better go and head to bed, now, it is getting late, and I have an early start tomorrow, I love you and miss you always".

"Love you too, bye darling".

You hang up the phone and turn the TV on for a couple of hours until you begin to fall asleep and decide to head off to bed.

As you awake the next morning, for a moment you find yourself confused by your different surroundings, once you find your bearings, you decide to get up and get ready to explore the city of Auckland.

On your way out of the apartment, you stop at the reception desk and ask the attendant where to find some breakfast, you are directed to a lovely little café just down the street. As you enter the café, you are surprised to see Derrick sitting at a booth in the corner, reading the paper, drinking a steaming cup of coffee, and enjoying pancakes.

Just as you decide to head over to say Hi, he looks up and spots you, a smile appears on his face, and he waves you over to join him.

"Good morning, Derrick, Great minds think alike by the looks of it?"

"Absolutely, how are you this morning Angela? you have to try these pancakes, they are awesome!"

Just as you take your seat, a young waitress comes over,

"Good morning, Madam, what can I get for you today".

"Oh, I think I will have a serve of those delicious pancakes, and a hot chocolate thank you".

"Fine choice won't be too long Madam" the waitress hurries off to the kitchen to place your order.

"So, Derrick, what do you have planned for today?"

"Oh, I thought I would take in some of the city sights, there is a city tour bus apparently that takes you all to the main attractions which sounds interesting, What about you?" Derrick replies

"I don't know really; thought I would just walk around and take in some sights etc" you reply.

"Hey why don't we go on the tour bus together? sounds like fun, and we shouldn't get lost if we are on the tour" laughs Derrick.

"Ok, sounds like an idea" you reply and with that the waitress returns with your order.

As you take a bite of your pancake, your taste buds are met with immense decadence. "Oh wow, these are so good, and with the cream, just perfection," you look at Derrick smiling.

"See I told you so" he replies chuckling.

After finishing breakfast, you and Derrick get ready to join the sightseeing tour. The tour bus is an open top double decker, you and Derrick take your seats and begin to take in the views. The tour bus winds its way through the streets of the city, you pass the Auckland Museum, and soon the Sky Tower comes into sight. The tour bus stops and allows time for exploration. You and Derrick make your way to the top of the tower and are mesmerised by the awesome views from the top. Luckily you have your phone with you and take as many photos as you can from all angles.

The tour finishes with a trip to the Mount Eden, another avenue to take in the wonderful scene from the top.

It is early evening when the tour bus returns you both to your accommodation building. Derrick asks, "Hey Angela, do you want to grab dinner again at Alessandro's?"

"Why not, it was lovely last night" you reply, and you both make your way to the restaurant, enjoying your meals as you reflect on the events and sights of the day.

As you finish your chocolate mousse for dessert, you look at your watch and realise it is nearly 8.00pm.

"Wow, Derrick it is nearly 8.00pm, I better head back to my apartment and call Chad, before I watch some TV and head to bed, there is a good movie I wanted to watch tonight".

"Gee time does fly doesn't it, I want to get back and call Bree too. What plans do you have for tomorrow?"

"I was planning on spending the day, preparing for my interviews this week, doing some grocery shopping etc, what about you?"

"I have some planning to do also, for the IT office set up, and you reminded me, I need to get some supplies from the grocery store also".

With that, you both pay for your meals and walk back to your apartment building. As the elevator stops at your floor, you turn to Derrick, "Thanks for today, it was so much fun, I am so glad you suggested the tour bus".

"No problem, Angela, it was good, wasn't it? the views were amazing".

"Thanks again Derrick, have a great night, oh by the way, did you want to go to the office together on Monday?"

"That's a great idea, say we meet here about 8.am on Monday, I can drive".

"That sounds great, 8.00am will be great, I will see you on Monday, have a great day tomorrow, night".

"Night Angela"

You both return to your respective apartments. You call Chad, and fill him in on your fantastic day sightseeing, watch the old movie you were waiting to see and then head to bed. The long day catches up with you and you drift off to sleep in mere seconds.

CHAPTER 7

*T*he sound of your alarm pierces through your sleep at 6.00am on Monday morning. You had a great day yesterday, preparing for your 5 interviews that you have scheduled for today. During the day yesterday, you were able to travel to the local supermarket and fully stock up on the groceries you need.

You shower and dress for the day ahead, after breakfast, you prepare your lunch and snacks for the day ahead at the office, grab your bag and head out the door to meet Derrick at the elevator.

"Good morning, Derrick, Are you ready for first day at the new office?"

"Morning Angela, yes, all ready to go, how did you go with your plans yesterday, all sorted for the day ahead?"

"Yes, had a great day yesterday, stocked up on supplies from the grocery store, planned for the interviews I have for today, so all ready and fresh for the day". With that, you both take the lift down to the basement, climb into Derrick's company car and set off for the new office.

A little while later, you both pull up outside the new office and it is beautiful, you are both amazed by the modern façade and lovely garden surrounding the building.

You both enter the building and make your way to the offices where you both will set yourselves up for the next two to three months.

You open your laptop and begin to prepare for the busy day you have planned. Despite being over in Auckland, you are still trying to keep tabs on your old position and helping the replacement staff member covering your old role.

Derrick starts to set up for his duties for the day, wiring up internet and power cables for the computers that will be arriving later that day.

As you are sitting in your office, answering emails from your colleagues back at the main office, suddenly you hear a commotion from down the hall where Derrick is working.

You hear him yell out "Aaahh, Oh no, crap".

You jump from your seat and rush out the door toward Derrick.

"Derrick are you ok? What happened"

You are met with "Help Angela, Aaahh".

As you reach the office where Derrick is working, you find him on the floor, with boxes, supplies and cables piled around him and he is holding his hand and there is blood pouring from his hand over him and the floor.

"Oh, my goodness Derrick, what happened?" as you rush to him.

"I was trying to install the cable for the computers here and my hand got caught and as I managed to release my hand, I overbalanced and fell and cut my hand on the stanley knife here" he responds shaking.

"Crap, Ok, let me find something to clean you up, you may need to go to the hospital for stitches."

You manage to find a first aid kit in the kitchen area, rush back with a wad of tissues and paper towels and begin to clean Derrick's hand.

Once you clear the blood, you see a large cut.

"Derrick, I am going to take you to the emergency department, you need stitches for that".

As you help Derrick up, you remember, that you have an interview scheduled in 20 minutes.

"Oh crap, I have an interview scheduled, crap, I will have to call the ambulance to come and get you".

"No, that is not necessary, I will be fine, just wrap it up in a bandage over there, I will be fine".

"No Derrick, you need medical attention for that, the cut is very deep, it will need stitches for sure".

Reluctantly, Derrick agrees, he sits on a chair, still in shock and pain as you call the local ambulance to come and take Derrick to the hospital for treatment.

Shortly after the ambulance arrives to take Derrick to the nearby hospital.

"Good job you called us" says the ambulance officer, "this is quite a nasty cut, it definitely will need medical attention".

As you watch Derrick climb into the ambulance, you realise that you need the keys to his car, so you can pick him after he has been attended to.

"Derrick give me your car keys, I will come and get you when you are done ok?"

"Thanks Angela, they are in my bag in the office".

You squeeze Derrick's remaining good hand, "You will be fine, I will see you in a little bit, ok?"

"Ok thanks" and with that you watch as the ambulance drives off.

As you turn around, you see a poor young girl standing in front of the building in shock, staring at you.

"Oh no, that is my first interview for today," Your reach out your hand to her, and notice you have some of Derrick's blood still on your hand and a little on your clothes.

You pull your hand back, "Oh, hi Tina is it?, how are you? thanks for coming in, I can explain what you just saw, please come in, let me clean up and I will be right with you".

Tina, still looking in shock, smiles at you and nervously follows you inside, you show her to the interview room and head to the bathroom to clean up.

As you return, Tina looks a little calmer.

"Sorry about what happened earlier, I can explain, my colleague had an accident while installing the computer cabling and cut his hand, he needed to go to the hospital for stitches."

"Oh, that is terrible, I hope he will be ok."

"Yes, I hope so, now let's get to the interview".

Just after 4.00pm in the afternoon, you finish up your last of the five interviews you had scheduled for today, you hear a message come through on your phone, when you look at your phone and see a message from Derrick,

It reads, "Hi Angela, it is just Derrick, everything is Ok, I needed 12 stitches! Are you able to collect me now? I am ready to leave when you can, thanks."

You respond, "Oh Derrick, so glad you are ok, I have just finished my last interview, I will leave now, see you soon".

You grab Derrick's belongings as well as your own and head to the car and travel the short distance to the local hospital to meet Derrick.

As you arrive, you enter the emergency department, after checking in a reception, you are taken to Derrick. He is laying on the hospital bed, looking very pale after his ordeal and his hand heavily bandaged and in a sling.

He looks up and you and smiles. "Hi Angela, thank goodness you are here to take me home, I am ready to get out of here".

"Hi Derrick, how are you feeling?"

"I am ok, I needed 12 stitches, luckily, I missed important arteries etc, they have given me some pain killers, so I am pretty tired and just want to leave now".

Derrick climbs off the bed and follows you out of the hospital.

On your way back to your apartment building, you turn to Derrick and ask "Hey Derrick, I was going to make a simple pasta for dinner tonight, do you want to join me for dinner? I am sure you won't be wanting to make anything for yourself."

"That would be lovely, thanks, I am getting pretty hungry actually".

"Great, sounds good".

Once you are back at your apartment, you help Derrick inside, sit him down on the couch, turn on the television and set about making dinner.

As dinner is cooking, you look over to Derrick to check on him, only to find that he has fallen asleep on your couch. You think to yourself, "Poor thing, he must be so tired after what he has been through today".

You let him rest until dinner is ready.

As you both sit down to eat, you turn to Derrick and ask "How is it? Is it OK?"

"Thanks Angela, it is lovely".

You sit and eat in silence until you are both finished.

You both make your way to the couch and chat about the events of the day and the interviews that you had.

Shortly after your conversation turns to your partners and married life. "So, Derrick, have you and Bree discussed having a family?" you ask.

"Oh yes, we have discussed it a lot, I would love to start a family now, but unfortunately Bree is not ready yet, she has recently received a promotion at her new job and is not ready to give that up just yet", Derrick looks at you and you can see the sadness fill his eyes.

"Oh, that would be hard, Chad and I want to have a baby as soon as possible, this promotion certainly has put a spanner in our plan right now, but as soon as I get back, we will be trying for a baby straight away".

"Oh, that is great for you Angela, hope it works out for you, I don't know when Bree will be ready, I have always wanted children, so it is hard for me that Bree wants to wait, If I am honest with you, we have had some disagreements about it. I had such a great loving family growing up, I just want to reciprocate it with my own children. I love Bree so much; I can't wait until she wants to have a baby".

"Hang in there Derrick, I know the pain you must feel, I am sure it will happen soon for you,"

You continue to chat for the next hour or so, and then Derrick looks at his watch and says "Wow, it is nearly 8.00pm, I think I will head back to my apartment, I am pretty tired, and I need to give Bree a call, fill her in on what has happened today", Derrick lifts his injured hand up. "Thanks for everything you did for me today and treating me to your lovely pasta dinner and conversation".

"No worries, Derrick, thanks for sharing dinner with me,

As you show Derrick to the door, you put your hand on Derrick's shoulder and say, "I am sure you won't be coming to the office tomorrow, you need to rest your hand".

"Yeah, the pain killers are wearing off a bit now, I will see how I feel in the morning after a good sleep tonight and let you know in the morning Ok".

"Ok no worries, don't push yourself ok, rest up".

"Goodnight and thanks again Angela"

"Goodnight Derrick"

As Derrick heads back to his apartment, you return to the kitchen, clean up and return to the couch and give Chad a call to check in and update him on the events of the day, after that you head to bed and fall asleep instantly after the massive day,

CHAPTER 8

*T*he next six weeks fly by, Derrick's hand quickly heals, and he has all the required cabling, and computer hardware installed and is working on the necessary software installation.

You have successfully interviewed all the required roles for the finance and marketing departments, and the teams are steadily growing. There are already six new staff members working in the new office with a further four finishing their required notice periods, all with expected starting dates within the next two weeks.

Training has successfully begun, and you are very confident with the strong team you have created.

Both Rick and Greta have been regularly checking in with you via online meetings and a very impressed with your efforts. Rick is expected to make a visit to the new office within the next two weeks to formally check in and welcome all the new staff members.

As you finish up for the final day of your 6th week and reflect on knowledge that you are now halfway through this assignment. You are filled with both relief and excitement that you are now so much closer to your assignment being concluded and soon will be able to plan to return home and return to Chad and your dream of having a child.

As you and Derrick return to the apartment building, you both reflect on the last six weeks and all that you have both achieved.

Just as the elevator reaches your floor in the apartment building, Derrick remembers a comedy show he watched recently and begins to recite the hilarious comedy skit, you find yourself laughing loudly as the elevator door opens and you step out, still laughing you place your hand on Derrick's arm and remark how funny that was.

As you turn to head to your apartment, a familiar face greets you. Chad is standing in the hallway outside your apartment. You squeal with excitement and run towards him jumping into his arms and kissing him excitedly.

"Oh, my goodness, Chad, what are you doing here?"

Chad stares in the direction of Derrick, and responds, "I got time off work, so I thought I would come and surprise you for the weekend".

"Oh, that is fantastic, I missed you so much".

Chad still has his eyes focused on Derrick, who is standing in the hallway watching the two of you.

Chad walks over to Derrick, holds out his hand, and says coolly, "Hi, you must be Derrick, I am Angela's husband Chad".

"Hi Chad, Yes I am Derrick, pleased to meet you, I have heard so much about you,"

They both shake hands; however, you are surprised to sense tension especially coming from Chad.

Derrick continues "I am glad you could make it over here; Angela has missed you so much, I will leave you two alone. I will see you back in the office on Monday, have a great weekend you two", giving you both a wink and cheeky smile as he turns to head towards his apartment.

You turn back to Chad, embracing him in another big hug, "Oh Chad, this is such a surprise, I am so excited you came, come let me show you my apartment".

Chad follows you into your apartment. As you enter you turn to look at Chad but can still sense some tension in him.

"Chad, what is wrong, are you alright?"

"You and Derrick seem to be getting along well" Chad remarks staring at you.

"Yes, Derrick is a good friend, we have been keeping each company while working here".

"Really, ok"

"What do you mean Chad? we work together, it has been great to have a friend here that understands what is like to miss you partner."

"Mmmm, Ok, you just seem pretty close, I was a bit shocked to see you both so close getting out of that elevator earlier".

"Seriously Chad, Derrick is just a friend, he told me about a funny show he watched recently, it was hilarious. There is absolutely nothing to be worried about, Now come here, I have missed you so much" you reach out and pull Chad closer for another passionate hug and kiss. You can feel the tension release from Chad as he reciprocates the kiss. He picks you up in his strong arms holding you tightly.

After a few minutes you pull away from each other, leading Chad to your windows, "Chad, you must see the views I have from my apartment windows, you can see the whole city. It is amazing."

Chad follows you and as he looks out over the city, he is very impressed with the view. "Wow, it is beautiful, I wouldn't want to leave this view", he pulls you close, and you both take in the view with his arms wrapped around you.

The two of you enjoy a lovely romantic dinner for two at the nearby Alessandro's restaurant, filling in each other on the recent events from back home and here in Auckland.

After dinner you return to your apartment and spend the night in each other's arms, reacquainting yourself with a passionate long awaiting love making session.

As you wake the next morning, you are still encapsulated in Chad's strong arms. Chad awakens and pulls you closer and envelops you in a passionate kiss. You explore each other's bodies again and climax with another erotic love making session.

The rest of the weekend is spent sharing with Chad the many wonderful sights of Auckland that you have enjoyed over the past 6 weeks.

Before you know it, your surprise visit from Chad is ending, he needs to head to the airport to catch his flight back home to return to work for the next shift.

A sense of dread fills your stomach as you drive Chad to the airport, after such a wonderful weekend together, you must prepare yourself to say goodbye to your beloved husband.

Chad checks in at the airport and fighting back tears, you walk with him to the departure gate. The boarding call for Chad's flight fills the airport and you know you must let him go, but you try to hold on to him for as long as you can. Eventually, you reluctantly let go, share in one more passionate embrace and kiss, then watch him disappear through the gate to board his plane back home. Tears escape your eyes and run down your face as you watch his plane take off and disappear into the night sky. You return to your apartment, excitedly remembering the wonderful weekend you have just had and prepare for bed.

It is your turn to drive to the office this week, so you leave your apartment and head to the elevator to meet Derrick.

"Good morning, Angela, do I need to ask, how was your weekend?" asks Derrick with a cheeky look and wink.

"Good morning, Derrick, the weekend was fantastic, it was such a huge surprise for Chad to visit, I showed him all the sights I have come to love around town, plus it was so great to spend time with him again" you respond with a smile.

"I bet it was!" Derrick responds with a wink, "I am really pleased for you, a bit jealous if I am honest, makes me miss Bree all the more, but I am so happy for you."

"Any idea of when Bree might come for a visit?"

"No, not yet, she has a big project at work she is working on, so she may not even get a chance to get over here unfortunately" responds Derrick and you can see the sadness fill his eyes.

CHAPTER 9

*T*he sound of an email coming through, interrupts your duties for the day. It is from Rick the CEO; you quickly open the email, and it reads:

"Hi Angela, Hope you are well and enjoying your time in Auckland, Greta has been keeping me updated on the wonderful progress you have been making with the setup of the new office. I will be coming over at the end of next week, to check in, and meet all the new staff personally. Can you please set up an office staff meeting for next Thursday.

All being well, your assignment in Auckland could be finished by the end of next week.

Catch up soon and thanks.

Rick Morgan"

You respond immediately to Rick advising that you have set up the meeting as requested, you begin to get excited, you could soon be heading home to Chad and be able to focus on your dream of having a baby.

The rest of the day passes without a problem and as you head back to the apartment building you discuss Rick's impending visit with Derrick.

Derrick also received a similar email, so you are both excited to think that you could both be headed home at the end of next week after close to three months away.

"Do you have any plans tonight, Angela? Do you want to grab a drink and maybe dinner to celebrate the ending of our assignment?" asks Derrick.

"That would be lovely Derrick, yes let's do that".

You both head to what has become your favourite restaurant, during your stay, Alessandros's.

As you enjoy your dinner you chat about everything that you have both achieved over the last three months, and your plans when you return home.

The next week flies by, all the required staff are now onboard and working efficiently, so you feel very confident that Rick should not have any issues when he arrives the next day. Before leaving for the day, you ensure that the office is all in order for Rick's visit and remind all staff of the important day ahead.

As both you and Derrick arrive the next day, you are surprised to find that Rick and Greta have both arrived. They greet you with big hugs and smiles.

"Good morning, Angela and Derrick, great to see you both, the office is looking fantastic, we are both so impressed" says Rick enthusiastically.

"Thanks Rick, that means a lot," you respond,

"Yes Rick, thank you, we are so proud of what we have achieved" chimes in Derrick.

"Rick, Greta, let me give you a tour of the building before the rest of the staff arrive" you gesture for Rick and Greta to follow you.

You lead them on the guided tour, and their faces light up with smiles, it is such a relief to see them so happy with the hard work you and Derrick have put in.

As your tour concludes, other staff members start arriving for the day.

The time arrives for the staff meeting, and you round up all the staff.

Rick heads to the front of the room, and introduces himself, welcomes everyone and sets about discussing the important mission statement for the company, and motivating everyone with his plans for the future. You notice all the staff smiling and can sense the excitement in the room.

After the meeting has finished, Rick sets about introducing himself personally to each staff member and getting to know them individually on a personal level. From your office, you can hear the staff chatting amongst themselves so impressed with Rick and so happy and motivated by his visit filling you with pride and excitement.

Rick makes his way to your office.

"Angela, do you have a moment to catch up?"

"Yes, certainly Rick, come in".

Rick sits down in front of you, with a huge smile.

"Well Angela, today has been fantastic, the staff you have found are wonderful and I feel confident that this office will be in great hands. I don't see any reason for you and Derrick to stay on site here anymore, any issues should be able to be handled via online meetings. we can arrange for you both to return home this weekend, You and Derrick have done a fantastic job".

Excitement and relief build in your body, "Thank you Rick, I am so happy that you appreciate what we have done."

"I will get Greta to organise your flight back home and let you know by the end of the day."

"Thanks Rick, I appreciate that".

Rick shakes your hand and leaves the office.

You can't wait to get back to your apartment that night and call Chad and let him know that you are finally coming home.

As promised at the end of the day, Greta confirms your flight details.

Later that night, you excitedly call Chad.

"Hello sweetheart how are you?" you excitedly ask.

Chad responds, "Hello sweetie, I am good, how was your meeting with Rick and Greta today?"

"I am coming home!" you exclaim with excitement.

"Really? , that is fantastic, When?"

"I have a flight leaving about 11am on Saturday, with the time differences should be home about 2.00pm"

"That is great news, I can't wait, I will be there to pick you up".

You continue to fill Chad in on all the events of Rick's visit.

Your final day in the office is tinged with both sadness and excitement. You have forged strong connections with the staff you have hired, and you will miss seeing them every day, however you know that you will be able keep in touch via online meetings, chats, and emails. You are also so excited to return home.

The next day, you and Derrick are ready to head to the airport, you collect all your belongings, bid farewell to all the apartment building staff that you have made close friends with over the past three months and head to the airport.

As your flight takes off, you take in the last sights of the city of Auckland and settle in for the trip back home.

Before you know it, your flight begins to descend into Brisbane, and the excitement begins to build in your stomach, soon you will be back in Chad's arms that you missed for so long.

After your flight lands, you gather your luggage and quickly head out to find Chad waiting for you. Amongst the crowd you spot him, you bound towards him and launch yourself into his strong arms, tears of happiness fill your eyes.

Chad catches you and pulls you in close and meets your lips with his in a strong passionate kiss. You hold the embrace for what seems like minutes not wanting to let each other go. As you finally pull away from each other, you see tears of joy forming in Chad's eyes.

"It so great to have your home darling".

"I am so happy to be back home, I never want to leave you again".

Chad picks up your luggage, "let's get home".

"Absolutely, let's get out of here".

As you head out of the airport you see Derrick and Bree equally happy to be reunited.

You give Derrick a smile and nod and continue with Chad to the car and then home.

CHAPTER 10

It has been six months since returning from Auckland, and you have settled easily into your new role as Training Manager at your new firm. You are enjoying combining training new and existing staff members as well as continuing with your previous finance manager role. As you are putting the finishing touches on the updated accounts training manual you have been working on since your return from Auckland, your thoughts are distracted by the sound of a message coming in on your phone. It is Hannah,

"Hi Angela, Are you busy tonight? I need to see you about something".

"Hi Hannah, of course I am free for you tonight, where do you want to meet?"

Hannah replies "Say we meet at the bistro Blue Horizons, around the corner from your place at about 6.30 pm?"

"That sounds great, Everything Ok lovely?"

"I will tell you about it tonight, can't wait to see you, enjoy the rest of your day lovely X".

"You too X"

The rest the afternoon drags on, as you think about your dinner with Hannah, it is unusual for Hannah to message you during the day like that and not fully explain herself. You try to think ahead to what she may be wanting to talk about, you are thinking perhaps it has to do with her engagement to Trevor, they got engaged shortly before your own wedding nearly ten months ago, perhaps they have finally set a date for their wedding. You tell you yourself, I bet that is it, you are really excited for her. Your mind begins to think about wedding ideas for Hannah, you jot down some ideas for flower decorations, music etc to discuss with her later that night.

Finally, the clock turns 5.00pm and you pack up ready to leave the office to head home to freshen up and head out to meet Hannah.

As you arrive at the Blue Horizon bistro, you look around but don't see Hannah yet. A waitress approaches you; you mention Hannah's name and she shows you to the reserved table, order a mocktail, and wait for Hannah.

Only ten minutes pass and Hannah rushes in looking flustered, you catch her eye and wave her over.

"Hey Hannah, are you ok, you look a bit stressed?", you stand and pull Hannah in for a big reassuring hug.

"Oh, hi Angela, yeah I am ok, just running a bit late" Hannah responds and takes a seat.

"What do you want to drink Hannah? I will go and get you a drink to help relax you, do you want a cocktail tonight?"

Hannah looks at you, "No, I am not really up to a cocktail, I think I will just have a soft drink, if you don't mind".

You look at Hannah, "That is not like you, is everything ok?"

Hannah looks at you and bursts into tears.

"Oh my god Hannah, what is wrong?" you pull Hannah in for another hug.

Hannah remains in your arms for a few minutes, seeming unsure how to respond, eventually she pulls away and returns to her seat, wiping the tears from her face, she draws a deep breath and looking nervous looks at you and says "Angela, I am pregnant, I found out this morning, I haven't told Trevor yet, we were not planning on this right now".

"Oh my god Hannah, that is amazing" you grab Hannah's hand and squeeze it. "Are you sure?"

"Yes, pretty sure, I missed my period, and I have been feeling really awful lately, I thought it was a stomach bug, I took a test, actually three tests, and they all came back positive".

"Oh wow, that is big news, I am so happy for you", as the news sinks in, mixed emotions begin to fill your mind. Of course, you are happy for Hannah, but secretly you are upset that you are not the one that is finally pregnant.

Hannah finally responds, "Angela, I am not sure how to feel exactly, it is such a shock, we were not even trying to get pregnant, we haven't even set a wedding date yet, I don't know how Trevor is going to react. I mean I know we definitely want children; I just thought it would be a bit further into the future you know".

"Hannah, I know it is not exactly planned, but this is great news, I am sure Trevor will be over the moon when you tell him, I am so happy for you, wow this is a surprise, certainly not what I expected you to tell me, I actually thought that you and Trevor had finally set a wedding date and that is what you were going to tell me"

"No, we have both been a bit busy, and just enjoying being together, we hadn't really discussed setting a wedding date yet, we were not in a rush, we were happy to have a longer engagement, save some money and have the perfect wedding you know, everything is messed up now" Hannah responds, and you can see the tears forming in her eyes again. She starts to get anxious again, "Oh no, I will end up being a pregnant bride, I don't want that, Oh Angela, it is all going wrong" tears start rolling down her cheeks again.

"Hannah, it will be ok, just try to relax and let's order some dinner and we can talk things through and sort things out", you hand Hannah a tissue and she nods.

You both sort out your orders and wait for the meals to arrive. Hannah is looking and feeling a bit calmer now.

"So, lets discuss the wedding aspect, there is no hard rule that you must get married before you have the baby, so therefore, you do not necessarily have to be pregnant bride, you can wait until after the baby is born do you think?" you ask Hannah.

Hannah thinks for a bit, and then responds, "I guess you are right; we could wait until the baby is born,"

Your dinner arrives, as you eat, you question Hannah, "So I know it is still really early, but you are excited about the baby, aren't you? it is such a blessing".

 "Of course, I am happy, as I said earlier, it was such a shock, I was not expecting this right now, but I am getting used to the idea, and actually I am getting excited about it" Hannah responds with a smile.

"So will you tell Trevor tomorrow?"

"Yes, I will, take him out to dinner to his favourite restaurant and tell him over dinner".

"That sounds like a great plan, oh, we have to go baby shopping, oh how exciting" you smile at Hannah excitedly.

"Woah, slow down lovely, I only found out this morning, and have to tell Trevor first" smiles Hannah.

"Ok, but I can't wait till we can go, there is so much you will need".

"Oh, don't remind me" replies Hannah, rolling her eyes.

After you both spend the next couple of hours chatting about the pregnancy and work, Hannah turns to you and says "I have to go home now, it has been a huge day, and I am beat, thank you love, you have helped calm me down, I can always count on you to help, I love you" Hannah pulls you in close.

"My pleasure love, I am always here for you, you know that".

As you reach your cars, Hannah looks at you, "Thanks again Angela, you helped me so much, Good night".

"Good night, Hannah"

As Hannah gets into her car, she looks at you and says, "You will be next to get pregnant, and our children will be able to grow up together".

"I hope so Hannah, Good night".

As you arrive home, your emotions start to build inside you, you are obviously happy for Hannah, but devastated that it is not you and Chad that are expecting a baby.

Tears begin to form in your eyes, as you settle into bed for the evening, the tears that have building release and you cry yourself to sleep.

As you wake up the next day, your mind remembers the night before and Hannah's big news. Chad is due home soon, and you can't wait to tell him the news.

After crawling out of bed, you freshen up for the day and as it is the weekend, you begin your household chores.

Shortly you hear the door open, and Chad appears, you rush to him and throw your arms around his neck and plant a passionate kiss on his lips. Chad pulls you close and deepens the kiss. A few moments later, you both pull away, "Hello sweetie, wow that was a wonderful welcome home" Chad exclaims.

"Hello darling yes, I missed you, excited you are home, and we can have the whole weekend together now. How was your shift? How was Trevor?"

"The shift was ok, there was a house fire we had to attend, poor family lost everything" Chad responds.

"Oh, that is terrible, is everyone safe?"

"Yes, luckily they were not at home at the time," he looks at your quizzingly, "Why were you asking about Trevor specifically? you have never asked about him like this before?"

"Oh, I was just curious, I had dinner with Hannah last night and it was interesting" you respond trying to hold back a smile.

"Interesting how? You are acting a bit strange, is something going on?", Chad asks with raised eyebrows as he plonks himself on the couch, removing his shoes to relax.

You join Chad on the couch, "Yes, there is something I am busting to tell you, As I said I had dinner with Hannah last night and she had massive news".

"Have they finally set a wedding date?" Chad interjects.

"No, not yet. Hannah is pregnant!"

"Wow that is huge, Trevor didn't say anything on shift" replies Chad with a puzzled look.

"That is because he does not know yet, well he will by the end of today, Hannah only found out herself yesterday and hadn't had a chance to talk to Trevor yet".

"Oh, so she told you first?"

"Yes, she was in shock and needed to debrief with me first before she told Trevor".

"Wow, that is great for them, how is Hannah feeling?"

"Apart from being in complete shock, it wasn't expected, she is feeling a bit sick which is expected, how do you think that Trevor will react?"

"I reckon he will be so happy; he has mentioned to me how excited he will be to be a dad one day, I see him with the kids when we do our school training sessions, he is a natural and the kids love him too".

"Oh, that is good, Hannah was bit worried as it was not exactly planned to happen right now".

"I am really pleased for them both, it is great news" Chad says as he looks deep in thought.

"Are you ok?" you ask.

"Oh yes of course" replies Chad, "I guess if I am truthful, I am a little jealous, I wish it was us that was pregnant", Chad pulls you closer.

"Yes, I know what you mean, I wish it was us too, I know it sounds awful, but I was a little angry last night, Hannah and Trevor were not even trying and they are pregnant, and we have been trying for the past ten months since we got married and nothing, it is not fair is it?"

"Yeah, I know what you mean, it will happen for us too eventually," Chad covers your mouth with his and kisses your passionately, while stroking your hair.

The rest of the day is spent attending to household chores, while Chad catches up on some sleep from his shift.

CHAPTER 11

*T*he next morning after you awake your mind rushes straight to thoughts of Hannah, wondering how she went telling Trevor the big news last night. You grab your phone and decide to send her a text.

"Morning Hannah, just checking in to see how last night went with Trevor, cannot wait to hear all about it. Take care, love you."

You snuggle back into Chad's strong arms, and your mind begins to think about the moment that you can finally tell Chad that he is going to be a father, you have run through the conversation and scenario over and over in your mind. You want to plan a special meal with all Chad's favorites and then surprise him with a special present, of a baby onesie with the words "Dad, you are my number 1" written on it. The smile on your face soon turns to anguish, as you cannot wait for that day to come, you ask yourself, why is it not happening yet?

Chad suddenly stirs and awakens from his sleep, pulling you into his arm tightly and kisses the back of your neck. "Good morning lovely, what are you thinking about."

You turn to face him, returning his kisses, shaking the thoughts from your mind you respond, "Good morning, I was just thinking about Hannah, I hope she is ok."

"I am sure she will be fine; Trevor is bound to be surprised, but he will be excited," Chad replies, and then covers your mouth with his and kisses you passionately as he begins to caress your body tenderly.

You feel the heat build in your body and escape into the passion of the moment, focusing only on Chad, and the pleasure that is to follow.

After your both have reached the height of ecstasy, you remain entwined in each other's arms regaining your breath and then begin to think about your plans for the remainder of the day. You have planned to meet up with Chad's brother and his wife for brunch.

"What time is it now?" you question Chad.

He looks over to his phone and sees that it is just past 8.30am, "I guess we better get up soon and get ready to meet Simon and Mary for brunch."

"Yes, true, we don't want to be late, it takes a while to drive over to their place."

"Yes, exactly, I will go and shower first, unless you want to shower together?" Chad looks at you questioningly.

You are about to respond when your phone buzzes with a message., You grab your phone, and see it is from Hannah. "Oh, it is from Hannah, you go ahead, I will come in shortly."

Chad leaves the bed and heads to the shower, and you quickly open the message from Hannah.

"Hi Angela, I will fill you in on all the details later, Trevor was surprised but so excited, I am so relieved, he is being so sweet, fussing already, can we catch up tomorrow, we are spending the day together, talking about and planning for the baby,"

You respond, "Oh Hannah, that is such great news, yes, we can catch up tomorrow after work, cannot wait to get all the details. Have fun planning for the baby, love you X."

The next day, you are sitting in your office trying to concentrate on the set tasks, but your mind keeps wandering to Hannah, and thinking about how lucky she is. Finally, the clock ticks over to 5pm and you are ready to leave and head over to Hannah's house to catch up.

Hannah greets you with a big smile and her traditional bear hug. She looks so happy and relaxed now, you are so happy for her, as you sit to enjoy the dinner, she has prepared for you both, she begins to fill you in on breaking the baby news to Trevor. She tells you how she decided to take him to one of his favorite restaurants, and how nervous she was to tell him, but ended up just blurting out the news. Trevor reacted initially by placing his hands over his face, in shock and then bursting into a huge smile, excitedly hugging Hannah with tears forming in his eyes. They spent the rest of the dinner talking about the baby and planning all the items they needed to get.

You hug Hannah and tell her how happy you and Chad are for her and Trevor and finish the evening with dessert and make plans to go baby shopping together the next weekend.

The rest of the weekend flies by and you meet Hannah at the local baby supplies store and start to research all the items she will need. It is a chance for you to also research all the items that you want to get when you are finally pregnant. Hannah and Trevor have decided to not find out the sex of the baby until he or she is born, so you begin to look at neutral tone items. As you begin looking at the clothing section, your eyes find a gorgeous little pink baby dress, with lace and ruffles, you fall in love with it, and cannot wait to show Hannah. "Hey Hannah, look at this, isn't this just gorgeous, I am definitely going to get this when Chad and I finally have a baby."

"Oh Angela, it is beautiful isn't it, so cute" Hannah smiles back "If I have a girl, I will come back and get one of those for sure."

You spend the next couple of hours checking out every corner of the shop, making notes on all the items needed and the prices.

"Wow, Angela, I knew having a baby would be expensive, but I am in shock at just how much we will need and the prices of everything, it is going to cost a fortune" says Hannah in surprise.

"Yes, it is a bit of shock at the prices, Chad and I will have to start saving now I reckon, or we can just borrow yours" you respond to Hannah with a wink, you both laugh jokingly as you leave the baby store and head to nearby café for a quick snack before heading home.

Three months later, you are sitting in your kitchen at home thinking about Hannah and how she is truly blossoming as her beautiful baby bump is growing. Soon you will need to begin to prepare a baby shower for her. As you are thinking about that, Chad enters the kitchen and heads to the pantry to grab a snack. Just then a thought enters your mind. "Chad, do you think we should see a fertility specialist?" you ask Chad.

With his back still facing you, "What, why?" Chad responds with a shocked voice. He turns around to you and looks at you with surprise.

You respond, "Well, we have been married for nearly a year now, and still not pregnant, do you think there is something wrong with one of us,"

"No sweetie, I think it will just take time, there is no need to involve a doctor right now" Chad responds still in shock.

"But why haven't we gotten pregnant yet, we have been trying for so long, it should have happened by now, there must be something wrong," you feel tears welling in your eyes.

"No sweetie, I think you are putting too much pressure on yourself and overthinking the situation, you just need to relax, and it will happen."

You snap back at him "How long do we have to wait? Don't you want a baby now?"

"Of course, I do Angela, you know that, but I think you need to chill a bit, you are stressing about it, and you just need to relax, you are focusing too much on getting pregnant, it is getting quite stressful to be honest, having our sex life regulated by the baby schedule, it is so regimented."

"Oh really, I haven't heard you complaining before." you snap back.

"Well, I am now, I don't like having to be told to only have sex at certain times of the month, as it is best to conceive, there is no fun to it anymore."

"Oh really, Ok, I thought it was our dream, obviously not your dream."

"Angela, it is still my dream, but I want it to be natural,"

You feel anger rising inside you and feel the need to just escape the situation, you respond to Chad, "I need to get out of here, I am going out" you grab your bag and head for the front door.

"Angela, where are you going?"

"Out" you snap back.

As you slam the door behind you, you hear Chad call after you, "Angela, calm down come back."

As soon as you get into your car, you feel the floodgates open and tears begin to flow down your cheeks as you head to the local beach, to sit and watch the waves to try and calm down. You are still incredibly angry and cannot believe that Chad implied that you were obsessing about becoming pregnant. It has always been your dream and you just want it to be your turn to be pregnant and experience what Hannah must be feeling.

After a while of sitting and thinking, you finally feel calm enough to return home.

As you enter the front door, you are not sure if Chad is still angry. You eventually find him in the study playing a computer game. "Hey, you have come home" Chad says calmly not even looking up from his game.

"Yes, I am sorry about storming out earlier, I just had to get out of the house for a bit, Sorry."

Chad stops playing his game and looks at you, "Ok, can we talk about things calmly now then?"

You nod in response and reach out your hand to grab his and pull him up out the chair for a cuddle, "I am sorry Chad."

"Ok, Angela, let's talk about thing calmly now" Chad says as he grabs your hand and heads towards the couch in the lounge.

He continues "Ok sweetie, I am sorry if I upset you earlier, I didn't mean to, I was just in shock that you suggested wanting to see a fertility specialist, I am sorry if you felt I wasn't listening to you."

"Thanks Chad, I appreciate it, I am just scared that it is not happening for us yet."

Chad pulls you in close, "I know sweetie, but without wanting to upset you again, I think you are putting too much pressure on yourself, you need to relax and just let things happen naturally, like Hannah and Trevor," Chad says, smiles and winks at you. You smile back at him and rest your head on his chest.

Chad continues "Sweetie, while you were gone, I thought about things, how about this for an idea, if you can try and relax and not focus so strongly about getting pregnant to a predetermined schedule, then if we still don't have any success in say the next six months, then we can think about seeking medical advice, how does that sound?"

Still resting your head on Chad's chest, you respond, "Ok, your plan sounds ok, I will try and relax a bit."

"Great, so we are good then?" Chad says as he lifts your head to look at you with smile. "Of course, I am sorry" you respond.

"Great" says Chad as he pulls you closer for a deep kiss and hug.

CHAPTER 12

*T*wo weeks later, you are sitting in your office finishing up the financial reports for month end when the familiar sound of an email draws your attention. The email is from Rick, he is calling a compulsory marketing and finance department meeting in an hours' time. You know that the company has been in talks with a new multinational company to undertake a new marketing program for their new skin care product line, you wonder if the meeting has something to do with that.

An hour later, you join your colleagues in the large meeting room and wait for Rick and Greta to arrive. A little while later Rick enters the room with Greta following him. Rick makes his way to the front of the room and calls everyone to attention, the room falls silent and focuses on Rick.

"Hello everyone, I have called you all here today to discuss the outcome of our recent tender submitted to "Simply Yours" for their new cosmetic range advertising campaign. Well, after lengthy discussions, I can confirm that our tender has been accepted."

The room erupts with cheers and claps.

As the room quietens, Rick continues "Yes, it is fantastic news, and now the work really begins, we must come up with the sales pitch by the end of the month, which is just three weeks away. So next week, I will be organizing initially a day long collaboration session in the conference room at San Anthony's Conference Centre. We need to brainstorm an idea concept, if we need longer than one day, we will continue until it is set. I don't need to tell you how important this campaign is, it will set up our business for the rest of the year at least. I will send you all details to your emails by the end of the day. Please start thinking about marketing concepts now, I also need you all to concentrate on your other jobs so they are in a state that can be left on hold for at least one day if not more.

So, are there any questions?

No one has any to raise at this point.

"Ok, great, as I said, collaboration seminar details will be sent by the end of the day, Thanks for your time, chat again soon, Thanks," and with that Rick leaves the room.

As you all leave the meeting room, all your colleagues look at each other with excitement mixed with anxiety as the gravity of the new project starts to dawn down on them all.

The next week is full of ensuring that all your current projects and tasks are completed to a standard where they can be left for short time while you collaborate on the new project.

The collaboration day has arrived and as you arrive at the conference room, you find all your fellow colleagues arriving, and you are all eager to begin the new and exciting project.

Shortly after Rick arrives and addresses the group.

"Welcome all, great to see you all, are we all ready to nut out an awesome unique sales pitch for Simply Yours new cosmetic line?"

You all answer "Yes" enthusiastically.

"Great, that is what I want to hear" responds Rick.

He continues to discuss the plan for the day and the brief that has been provided by Simply Yours.

Then you are separated into smaller focus groups and start collaborating.

Hours later, you all meet again and present your ideas to the group.

After deliberation and minor adjustments by the early afternoon, you all feel that you have reached a successful pitch.

The idea is to present the marketing concept "Be yourself" for the cosmetic line, allowing consumers to focus on a natural look for their cosmetics.

All your colleagues including Rick and Greta are more than satisfied with the pitch, and strongly feel it will be a winner. The head of the marketing team has the job of collating the pitch into a report which Rick will present to the client at the beginning of the next week. You will be required to contribute figures in relation to marketing costs, so you will need to concentrate on that aspect tomorrow to include in the report.

Rick is so impressed with the pitch that he allows you and your colleagues to take the rest of the day off and start fresh the next morning.

As you leave the venue, you realise that you are very close to Chad's fire house, so decide to take a detour and drop in to surprise him. Luckily, as you arrive at the firehouse you notice that all the firehouse vehicles are on site, so you are assured that Chad would be on site.

After entering the firehouse and chatting to several of Chad's colleagues you reach his office and find Chad concentrating on some paperwork. You decide to sneak in and surprise him, you sneak up behind him, placing your hands over his eyes and planting kisses on his neck and cheeks. Chad jumps with surprise and swings around with a smile on his face. "Hi sweetie, what are you doing here?'

"The marketing session finished early, I was close by and thought I would pop in for a visit".

"Oh great, how did your session go? Did you come up with a plan"?

"Yes, and Rick loves it, he is going to present it to the client early next week, so we will wait and see, how is your shift going today"?

"Good, luckily it has been very quiet, so getting caught up with the paperwork, glad you are here, I can take a break" Chad stands up and pulls you in close, encompassing you in his strong arms and covering your lips with his.

You kiss him passionately back, rubbing your hands up and down his back and moving around to his chest and feeling his strong muscles under his shirt.

A sneaky thought enters your mind, you pull away from Chad and close and lock his office door, closing his window blinds, turning to Chad, with a cheeky smile, wrapping your arms around his neck as you pull him towards the bed that is in his office that is for him to use when on the 24-hour shifts.

"What are you doing Angela" Chad responds as he follows you to the bed.

"I think you know" as you place your hands on his chest and begin to unbutton his shirt pulling it out of his pants and throwing it on to the floor, exposing his well-defined chest.

"We are in my office, what if the call alarm goes off?" Chad responds smiling.

"Well, we better be quick then" you wink back at Chad, as you remove his belt and begin to pull down his pants.

"Oh Angela, you are naughty" Chad responds unzipping your dress exposing your back.

Minutes later you are both naked on his bed enjoying a spontaneous love making session, filling each with passion, feeling the excitement and intensity of each other.

As you both regain your breath and redress yourselves, you hear a voice outside in the corridor asking another "Have you seen Lieutenant Williams?"

"I think he is in his office".

Chad jumps up, "Quick, someone is coming".

Just then there is a knock-on Chad's door, as you and Chad smooth your clothes and hair, Chad responds to the knocking, "Hang on a sec, I will be right there".

Chad takes one last look at you and satisfied opens the door,

"Hello Baxter, how can I help you" Chad asks trying not to draw attention to what has just happened in his office.

You see a young cadet called George Baxter, standing in the doorway, he looks at both of you, "Oh Lieutenant, sorry to bother you, I can come back if you are busy" George responds.

"No George is it, it is fine, I was just leaving, Nice to see you, the Lieutenant is all yours" you smile at George and Chad, grab your bag, and start to leave. As you leave, you give Chad a kiss, and a hug, whispering in his ear, "That was close" smiling as you pull away. "See you tonight darling".

"Thanks for popping in, that was a great surprise, see you tonight sweetie."

With that you smile at George and leave the firehouse and return home.

Later next week, Rick calls another staff meeting for both the finance and marketing departments. As you all make your way into the meeting room, you all know that the pitch you worked hard on has been presented to the client, and you all anxiously await Rick to advise if it was successful. Minutes later, Rick arrives and makes his way to the front of the room, the room falls silent, focusing intently on Rick awaiting the result.

"Hello again everyone, glad you are all here. As you all know, I meet with the management team of Simply Yours and presented our pitch and...." He pauses for drama before continuing "They loved it and want us to run with this project".

Cheers and claps fill the room.

Rick announces the finance and marketing teams that will focus on the project. "Angela, you will head the finance team for this project ensuring that costing is accurate, and the budget is adhered to, Kate and Justin will assist you", You are excited to be trusted with such an important project and cannot wait to start with your team,

Two weeks pass and as you wake to get ready for a busy day at work, you start to feel different to usual, your stomach feels nauseous, and you rush to the bathroom and empty the contents of your stomach. "Ooh that's not good" you tell yourself just as another wave of nausea comes over you.

As you recover and clean yourself up, you try and think what may have caused that, you don't recall eating anything out of the ordinary the previous night.

Still feeling nauseated you decide to stay home from work as you are worried about having a stomach bug and not wanting to pass anything on to your fellow colleagues.

After calling Greta to advise of your absence, you climb back into bed still feeling unwell, your mind wanders and suddenly your eyes open widely, "oh my goodness", you jump out of bed, run to your cycle spreadsheet, and realise that your period was due over a week ago. So many thoughts run through your mind, "I am not usually late, but I have been busy, finalising the budget for the Simply Yours project as well as dealing with some other project issues. "Am I late because of stress? Or could I finally be pregnant?"

Rushing to the bathroom, your heart is pounding, you pull out a pregnancy test. After waiting the three minutes you are so nervous to look at result. You pick up the test, tears building in your eyes, shaking nervously, closing your eyes, you pull the test closer and force your eyes open to look at it. Focusing on the test, you gasp in shock, it reads "Positive" Still shaking you hold the test in your hand as you decide to take another test to confirm the result. When that comes back positive as well you kneel on the floor of the bathroom crying, scared to believe it is true, finally your dream has come true. Although still feeling nauseated, you return to bed, still scared to believe the results, you decide to make an appointment at your doctors to confirm the result,

The doctor's appointment arrives and your doctor knowing how important having a baby is to you, is so happy to confirm your pregnancy result, excitement and relief takes over and you cannot help but hug your doctor, wiping away tears, you leave your doctor on a high with a prescription for some medication to help with the nausea recommendations for prenatal vitamins and a referral to an obstetrician.

As you arrive home, you start preparing the dinner you have planned for this occasion.

The time arrives when Chad should be arriving home. Dinner is cooking and you have the box with the baby onesie ready to surprise Chad.

Time ticks over, Chad is later than usual, he must be busy on a job, luckily dinner is a casserole, so it won't spoil if it is left longer.

Another hour passes and still no sign of Chad, you turn off the casserole as you begin to worry, it is a bit unusual for Chad to be this late and not send a message or call.

Suddenly the doorbell rings startling you, you open the door to find Chad's fire chief Wally Johnson standing on the front doorstep.

"Wally, why are you here, where is Chad?" you ask as your voice begins to quiver.

"Angela, there was an accident, Chad is in the hospital, I am sorry, Come I will take you to the hospital."

You begin to shake, place your head in your hands, "Oh no, is he ok? What happened?"

"Come with me and I will fill you in on the way to the hospital".

In the car, Wally begins to fill you in on what happened to Chad. "We were attending a factory fire, it was a double story building Chad was on the top floor checking for victims, and suddenly the top floor gave way, and he fell."

You gasp in horror,

Wally continues, "We rushed to him, and pulled him out, the ambos checked him, he appears to have dislocated his left shoulder and broken his left leg in the fall and has a nasty gash on his side and other cuts from the fall. He was unconscious and rushed to hospital for surgery".

"Oh my god" you exclaim in tears.

The rest of the trip to the hospital seems to take an eternity.

So many thoughts are rushing through your head, you are scared for Chad, is he going to be alright? How can this be happening just as you find out that you are pregnant, and Chad and your dream has finally come true.

Eventually you arrive and as you enter the hospital, all Chad's team are there waiting, ready to support you and Chad. As you enter, they all rise and greet you with hugs and well wishes.

Thanking each of them, your eyes finally meet Hannah's, she is there with Trevor, she pulls you in tightly for a hug, tears are in her eyes as she says "Angela, I am here for you, Chad will be Ok".

"Thank you, Hannah, I need to find his doctor".

Just as you say that a doctor appears, and heads towards you.

"Mrs Williams?" he asks.

"Yes, that is me, is Chad Ok, can I see him?" you respond anxiously.

Chad's team gathers behind you, all waiting to hear the doctors' words.

"Chad is still in surgery now; he has dislocated his left shoulder and has serious fractures in his left leg which we are stabilising. He also has a serious gash to his left side after falling on some debris. We are repairing that damage now. He also has some other cuts and bruises and some minor exposure burns. He is a very lucky man, and lucky his team got to him so quickly. We expect him to make a full recovery, but it will be a long road as the leg fractures are multiple and quite serious. I need to get back into theatre, I will be back to let you know when you can see him".

"Thank you doctor".

Although you feel relieved, you are still very scared, you turn to Hannah, and she hugs you as your tears start to flow.

"See I told you he will be alright, he is strong" Hannah says trying to be comforting.

The rest of his team are relieved to hear the news.

You turn to them and thank them for being here,

"Thank you, all guys, thanks for getting Chad out and for being here, you don't need to stay though".

They respond in unison, "we are not going anywhere".

Wally places his hand on your shoulder looking at you, "He is our brother, we are not going anywhere until he is out of surgery, and we know he is safe".

"Thank you, Wally, thank all of you".

Hannah leads you to a seat and sits next to you as you wait for the doctor to return.

She offers to get you some food or water, but you can't stomach anything.

CHAPTER 13

*T*ime appears to stand still as you wait for the doctor to reappear to update you on Chad. Hannah stays by your side, holding your hand. All the while, she tries to engage you in small talk to try to keep your mind off your worries, unfortunately it does not work and all you can think about is Chad, and what he is going through. Chad's colleagues remain at the hospital the whole time, their 24-hour shift finished an hour ago, some are sleeping in the waiting room chairs, others are just sitting waiting, but they will not budge until they know that their brother is safe,

Finally, you notice the doctor appear, he searches the room until he finds you. You jump from your seat, Hannah closely follows, the room all focuses their attention on you and the doctor.

"Doctor how is Chad?" you ask anxiously.

The doctor responds, "Chad is out of surgery and is in recovery, we have been able to fix the dislocation in his shoulder. We have been able to stabilise the fractures in his femur and tibia. We have successfully repaired the injury to his side, he has an injury to his spleen. As I mentioned earlier, he is a very lucky man".

"Oh, thank you Doctor, Can I see him please" you plead with the doctor, tears filling your eyes.

"He has just come out of surgery, and still quite sedated. Let us get him settled in a ward, and we will come and get you, should be about 15 minutes".

You nod at the doctor, thanking him again. As the doctor turns to leave, you turn to Hannah and she embraces you, the emotions of the day reach the surface and you break down in Hannah's arms.

"It's Ok Angela, it is good news, Chad is going to be Ok, he is tough, he will get through this, we are all here for you and Chad" says Hannah.

"Absolutely, Angela, we are all here for you and Chad, whatever you need just ask" says Wally as he places a supportive hand on your back.

As you turn to face Wally, you see all his colleagues standing, smiling and relieved to hear the news of Chad.

In unison they all respond "Here Here"

You are so thankful and feel the warmth of the firehouse family around you.

A short time later, a nurse comes out to the waiting room, scanning the room, she asks "Mrs Williams?"

"Yes, that is me" you respond as you walk towards her.

The nurse smiles at you, "We have settled Mr Williams into a ward now, we can allow you to see him, please remember, he is still heavily sedated."

Wally, Trevor, Hannah, and the rest of the team smile at you and nod for you to go ahead to see Chad.

Wally calls after you, "Give him our best, tell him his firehouse family are here for him".

You follow the nurse down the corridor, the nurse opens the ward door and your eyes land on Chad in the hospital bed, you rush to his side, he is unconscious, but you grab his hand, squeezing it, with your other hand, you caress his hair. Trying to hold back tears, you whisper to Chad, "Darling, I am here, you are going to be OK".

You sit down next to his bed, still holding his hand.

A little while later, the nurse returns and says "Mrs Williams, he is going to be unconscious for a while, perhaps you want to go home for a rest."

"No, I don't want to leave".

"I understand, but there is nothing you can do for him right now. You are looking a little pale, are you feeling, Ok?"

"Yes, I am fine, it has just been a big day, I want to stay with him:

A little while later, Hannah comes in,

"Hey Angela, the nurse wanted me to come and see you, she is worried about you. I think you should come and stay with us tonight and we can let Chad rest, and we can come back tomorrow, there is nothing you can do for him tonight".

"What if he wakes up and I am not here?" you reply.

"The doctors have him heavily sedated, they assure me he will not wake up tonight, come home and get some sleep and we can come back first thing in the morning Ok".

Looking at Chad, you reluctantly accept that you need to leave with Hannah, the events of the day, plus your pregnancy symptoms are building up and you are feeling nauseated. "Alright Hannah, I will go, but I want to be back here first thing in the morning please".

"You got it girl, come on let's go".

You stand and give Chad a kiss on the forehead. "Night Darling, I will be back tomorrow, I love you "

As you turn to leave with Hannah, nausea takes over, and you feel weak and nearly faint.

Hannah rushes to grab you as you steady yourself on Chad's bed. "Woah Angela, are you ok?"

"Yes, I think so, just been a big day".

Hannah supports you, "Come on let's go home, get something to eat and rest".

You smile at Hannah, grab her hand, and follow her out the door and as you reach the waiting room, you feel relieved that Chad's colleagues have also left to go home and rest.

The next day, you wake up at Hannah and Trevor's, the events of the previous day, hit you again, and tears begin to fill your eyes. As you get up and head out to meet Hannah, a wave of nausea hits you, you make it to the bathroom in time. After cleaning yourself up, as you leave the bathroom, Hannah appears with a questioning look on her face.

"Are you ok Angela, did I just hear you being sick?"

Looking at Hannah, you try to think how to respond, you are not ready to tell Hannah the truth right now, you want the first person you tell to be Chad.

"Hi Hannah, yes, I was a bit sick, I think it is just the stress of Chad".

"Ok, that makes sense, I thought it might have been morning sickness" Hannah responds jokingly.

You don't respond, instead you return to your room to finish getting dressed so you can get ready to return to the hospital to Chad.

As you approach the kitchen, Hannah offers you breakfast, your stomach is still not great, but you know you must eat something. "Thanks Hannah, my stomach is still a little weird, I think will just have some toast".

Straight after finishing your breakfast, you get ready to return to the hospital to check on Chad.

Once at the hospital, you rush to Chad's room just in time for him to begin to wake up, you hold his hand, smiling at him. Chad is still groggy but smiles back at you.

"Hello sweetheart, how are you feeling? You scared all of us" you ask Chad while caressing his hair.

Chad responds "Hi, I feel pretty tired and sore, but so glad to see you" he smiles weakly at you.

"Yeah, I am sure you are sore, you have a broken leg, had a dislocated shoulder, and a nasty injury to your side, you need to rest now, I am so glad that you are awake now".

"I am pretty thirsty; can you get me some water darling?" Chad asks.

"Of course, one second"

As you stand up to get Chad's water, the nausea and dizziness strike again and you almost faint.

Chad notices and questions you "Angela, what happened are you ok?"

Not wanting to tell him about the pregnancy like this, you respond smiling "I am fine, don't worry about me, you are the one we need to worry about".

"As long as you are sure, you looked like you were going to fall".

You get Chad's water and sit back down next to him, still feeling a bit weak and lightheaded, you try to push through and focus your attentions on Chad.

The doctor arrives on his morning rounds a little while later and is happy to see Chad awake.

"Good morning, Mr Williams, glad to see you are awake, how are you feeling today?"

"Morning Doc, you can call me Chad, you tell me, what happened yesterday? I only remember being in the factory checking for victims and I heard a crash and the next thing I know I am here".

"Well Chad, while you were in the factory, the first floor collapsed under you and you fell, you dislocated your shoulder, suffered multiple fractures to your femur and tibia, and as you landed, it would appear that you landed on some debris causing a large gash to your side and injuring your spleen, you also suffered minor abrasions and minor exposure burns. You are very lucky your team were able to get to you very quickly and rescue you."

Chad grimaces, "Wow, no wonder I feel like I have been hit by a truck as they say".

"Are you in any pain currently" the doctor asks.

"My side is pretty intense" Chad responds, the pain in his face is evident.

The doctor examines the area, and a serious look appears on his face, "There is more bleeding than I would have anticipated at this stage, let me call the nurse, we need to remove the bandage and have a closer look."

You and Chad look at each other with concern, and the doctor returns with a nurse. As they remove the bandage, the extent of the injury is clear, there is a large gash and blood is flowing from the wound.

"Oh dear" says the doctor, "It appears that the wound has reopened, we will need to get you back into surgery, flush the wound, check and restitch."

You grab Chad's hand, trying to be strong for him, but the pregnancy nausea, and events of the past day are overwhelming, and you can't hold back the tears.

Just then the nurse quickly returns to take Chad to surgery.

Still holding his hand, wiping tears from your eyes, "It's going to be ok sweetheart, I will be here waiting when you return." You kiss him on the forehead and the nurse wheels Chad out of the room back to surgery.

Hannah rushes into the room and pulls you in for a hug,

"It will be Ok lovely; the doctors and nurses will look after him".

You nod your head and the tears flow as Hannah tries to console you.

Hannah sits with you as you wait for news. "Hey Angela, do you want something to eat?"

"No thanks, I can't stomach anything right at the moment" you shakily respond as you stare intensely at the door waiting for the doctor to return.

"Ok, let me know if you change your mind" says Hannah smiling as she squeezes your hand.

Unsuccessfully, Hannah tries to engage you in small talk to pass the time, but all you can focus on is Chad.

After what seems like hours, the doctor finally appears and makes his way towards you.

"Doctor how is Chad?" you ask as you jump up from your chair.

"Hi Mrs Williams, it was a little tricky, but we have been able to find the source of the bleeding and repaired the damage. We flushed the wound, and increased his antibiotics as there were some signs of an infection forming. He is now in recovery and will be returning to his room soon".

"Thank you doctor, that is a relief, when can I see him?"

"He should be back in his room in about 30 minutes, but we still have him sedated".

"I just want to sit with him".

"I understand, I will have the nurse come and find you as soon as he is settled, Do you have any other questions for me".

"Are you sure he will be Ok now?"

"Yes, Mrs Williams I don't forsee any other issues with his recovery."

"Ok thank you Doctor".

The doctor smiles and leaves.

"That is good news Angela" says Hannah encouragingly.

"Yes, I just want to see him for myself" you reply anxiously.

"Understand, should not be too much longer".

Finally, the nurse appears, "Mrs Williams, Mr Williams is now back in his room, he is still sedated, but you are welcome to sit with him if you like".

"Yes, thank you, I need to see him" you respond as you follow the nurse to Chad's room.

"We will be here waiting for you Angela" Hannah calls after you. You turn and smile at Hannah as you head to Chad's room.

The nurse opens the door, and you rush into Chad's bedside, grab his hand and caress his hair, "Darling, I am here now, you will be fine now".

You sit next to Chad for the next 30 minutes and Hannah enters the room. "Hi lovely, how is he?" Hannah whispers.

"He is still sleeping; I am just relieved he is going to be ok".

"That is good, the nurse has told me that he is likely to be asleep for a while, come with me, and we can take a break and get some dinner?"

"I really don't want to leave him".

"Understand, but you have to eat, I will bring you back here as soon as we are done, and the nurse can call you if anything changes".

Reluctantly, you agree, you kiss Chad on the forehead, "I will be back soon darling, just rest, love you". You follow Hannah to a nearby restaurant, feeling relieved you are able to enjoy a meal with Hannah and Trevor.

As you return to Chad, you are relieved to see him awake, he is still very groggy, but he smiles as he sees you enter the room.

"Hi Darling, you are awake, how are you feeling? You had us worried" you ask as you make your way to his bedside.

"Hi Darling, I feel pretty tired still".

"Of course, you have had to have more surgery".

"Oh, ok" replies Chad yawning.

"Just rest Darling".

Chad closes his eyes and drifts off to sleep.

You sit with Chad, holding his hand, and Hannah enters the room, "How is he?" she asks.

"He is sleeping now" you whisper.

"Ok, do you want to come back home with Trev and me? We can let him rest, and I can bring you back here first thing in the morning".

"Ok, thanks Hannah, I am pretty tired, as long as we can return first thing".

"For sure" Hannah replies

You gently kiss Chad and follow Hannah out of the room.

The next morning as promised, Hannah brings you back to the hospital, you can't wait to get to Chad's room.

As you enter, you find him sitting up having a light breakfast.

"Hey Darling, you are looking better"
you say smiling.

"Hey, I am doing ok, still sore but not
as bad as yesterday, apparently the
doctor will be in on his rounds shortly.

As if on cue, the doctor knocks on the
door and enters smiling.

"Good morning, Chad, how are we
feeling today?"

"Hi Doc, I am still pretty sore and
wiped, but not as bad as yesterday."
Chad responds.

"Understandable, good there has
been some improvement, let me
have a look at the surgery site", the
doctor proceeds to examine the
wound and Chad's charts. "Good,
the site is looking better than
yesterday, so that is good".

"Oh good, how long will I have to be here before I can go home" Chad asks.

"You have had some serious injuries; I would expect you to be here for at least the next couple of weeks while we monitor your recovery, and you will have to be able to have adequate mobility before you are allowed home. So, Chad, you will be here for a while longer, lay back, relax, and recover, I will come back to see you tomorrow morning, reach out to the nurses if the pain becomes too intense or you need anything further Ok".

"Ok, thanks Doc" replies Chad

"Yes, thanks Doctor" you reply.

CHAPTER 14

*T*he next couple of weeks pass by so quickly, between working part days, travelling to the hospital to be with Chad as he recovers, as well as dealing with the constant morning sickness it all seems like a blur. You try to look after yourself, but your focus is on Chad and his recovery.

As you arrive to visit him, the doctor arrives for his daily check in, "Well Chad, how are we feeling today?" the doctor asks smiling.

"Hi Doc, I am feeling pretty good, my shoulder is much better now, still have a bit of pain in the left side", Chad gestures to his side with a little grimace. "I am slowly getting used to the crutches now".

"Oh, that is good news" replies the doctor, "Yes, your physio has advised that you are making good progress with your mobility, so that is a very pleasing result".

You smile warmly at Chad, "So Doctor, when do you think he will be able to come home?".

"Well, I would like to keep him in for one more night, but I think he should be ok to be discharged tomorrow morning" The doctor then turns to Chad, with a serious look on his face, "If I agree to let you go home tomorrow, you must promise to take things easy and continue with your physio exercises, Agreed?".

"Absolutely Doc, I just want to get out of here and get home".

"Ok, I will come by again first thing in the morning, and all being well, you can go home tomorrow, is that ok?" this time the doctor looks at you questioningly.

"Yes, doctor, that will be great, I will make sure he behaves" you give Chad a cheeky smile and squeeze his hand.

"Great, I will see you both tomorrow, I expect to be doing my rounds about 9.00am, so Mrs Williams, if you could be here around that time to collect Chad, that will be great, behave for the rest of the day Chad, and see you both tomorrow ok" says the doctor with a smile.

"No problem at all" you and Chad reply in unison.

As the doctor leaves, you look at Chad with a smile, "That is fantastic news, I can't wait to get you home and spoil you".

"I know" replies Chad with relief, "It will be so good to get home and back to you, plus it will be a relief that you want have to make the drive to the hospital every day that you have been doing, you have been looking so tired and pale the last couple of days, are you feeling, Ok?"

"Yes, darling I am fine, just been a big week is all", you still not ready to tell Chad the news of the pregnancy, while he is in the hospital, you want it to be special. Chad's birthday is coming up in a couple of days, so you want to wait to tell him then to make his birthday extra special. "With your birthday the day after tomorrow, it will be great to get you out of here and home by then" you respond.

"Yes, getting home to you, will be the best present I could ask for" Chad smiles.

You think to yourself "Well Chad, I have an extra special surprise which will top that".

After visiting with Chad for a while, you decide to leave, and head home to prepare for Chad's homecoming.

On the journey home, you call Greta to let her know the update on Chad, work have been so supportive since Chad's accident, allowing you to take as much time as you need to attend to Chad. Luckily, your job allows you to perform a lot of your duties from home, so you will be able to stay at home, look after Chad and keep up to date with work assignments. Greta is thrilled to learn that Chad will be coming home and is supportive of you working from home and requires you to check in via teams video meetings at least once a week, so that is one less pressure off you.

As you settle into bed for the night, you are filled with mixed emotions, you are excited to have Chad home, and finally be able to tell him your news, but you are also worried about his mobility until he fully recovers, and with dealing with your own sickness from the pregnancy, you worry if you can do it all on your own. Eventually you fall asleep.

The next morning, although still feeling unwell yourself, you push through and head to the hospital to collect Chad. You arrive just before the doctor, Chad is sitting on the edge of the hospital bed, dressed in tracksuit pants and sweater, eagerly anticipating being released and coming home. He reminds you of a young child eagerly awaiting Christmas morning. As you head to Chad, you smile "Good morning darling, you look set to leave" you give him a kiss and hug.

"Good morning, sweetie, yes, I can't wait for the doctor to get here and let me go home".

The doctor arrives shortly after, he is very pleased with Chad's recovery so far and signs the discharge papers. He hands you detailed instructions and follow up physio and medical appointment details.

A nursing assistant helps Chad into a wheelchair and follows you out to your car. You both thank the nursing staff on your way out.

As Chad gingerly gets into the car, he turns to you with a relieved smile, "Thank goodness I am out of there, let's go home".

After a short drive you both arrive home and to your surprise, Hannah and Trevor are there to greet you.

They rush to help you both out of the car and help Chad inside.

"Hey lovely, great to see you both, how did you know that Chad was coming home today?" you ask Hannah as she pulls you in for a hug.

"Trev rang Chad last night and he told us he was coming home today, so we came over with some shopping and food etc, we know you have been so busy you wouldn't have had time to shop etc, it was the least we could do, plus we wanted to welcome Chad home" Hannah replies as she turns to give Chad one of her hugs.

"Thank you, sweetie, that is so lovely," you respond, "let's go inside".

Trevor helps Chad inside to the couch, and you and Hannah head to the kitchen to unpack all the goodies that she bought over for you.

"Thank you so much for this Hannah, it is so appreciated".

Pregnancy emotions threaten to take over, and you feel tears forming in your eyes.

Hannah notices, and pulls you in for a hug, "Hey Angela, it is ok, you two have been through so much it was the least we could do."

You nod and manage to keep the tears at bay for now.

You both make a cuppa and return to the boys in the lounge.

Hannah and Trevor stay for a short time and then head off for a doctor appointment and ultrasound.

After they leave, you sit next to Chad on the couch and grab his hand "Darling, I am so relieved to have you home now, do you need anything?"

"I only need you sweetheart," as he pulls you close to his good side and kisses you deeply.

You both spend some time in each other's arms on the couch, watching some TV and even both drift off to sleep for a little while.

After waking up and having a bite to eat, it has been a big day and you are both exhausted and decide to turn in for the night.

Chad finds it hard to get comfortable but eventually drifts off to sleep, as you lay in his arms, you think about the next day, Chad's birthday, and the day you finally get to surprise him with the news he will soon be a father.

The next morning you awake, Chad is still asleep, he had a restless night at times, so you leave him be, and decide to get up and prepare the surprise for him.

You package up the baby onesie in the box and place a lovely bow on it and place it on the table ready for when he awakens. As you are in the kitchen preparing pancakes, you hear Chad make his way out of the bedroom to join you.

As he reaches the kitchen you turn to him and smile "Happy Birthday darling" you say excitedly

"Thank you, sweetie," he responds smiling as he makes his way to the table with his crutches. "Oh wow, is this for me?" he points to the box on the table.

"Yes, it is, but have your pancakes first, and then open the box".

As you both sit and eat the birthday breakfast, the excitement is building inside you. You clear away the dishes and then place the box in front of Chad.

"There you go, Happy Birthday Darling" and give him a big kiss and hug.

You take a seat next to him and anxiously wait for him to open the present.

He removes the bow, and gently removes the paper.

"Don't be careful, just get into it, I can't wait for you to open it" you say impatiently.

"Ok, give me a sec" says Chad.

He removes the lid and pulls out the onesie, reads it and then as the words "Dad, you are my number 1" register, he drops the onesie and looks at you with shock on his face.

"Oh my god, Angela, is this right, are we pregnant?" he exclaims.

Tears fill both your eyes and Chad's as you nod and get up and head to him.

Tears roll down his face and he holds you close.

Finally, he can mutter the words "Oh my god, this is fantastic, how long have you known?"

"I found out the day you had the accident."

"Why didn't you tell me sooner?" he questions.

"The hospital was not the place to tell you that, and we were trying to focus on your recovery."

He nods in agreement with you, pulling you in again for a deep kiss and hug.

"So how have you been feeling sweetheart?" Chad asks you as he holds you tight.

You respond "Truthfully, with everything going on I haven't really had time to think about it, the nausea is hard, and I feel pretty tired sometimes, but I struggle through, it will be easier now that you are home."

"Yes, I will look after you now," Chad responds pulling you in closer. After a little thought, he continues "It makes sense now, why sometimes when you came to visit me in the hospital, you looked so pale and tired, I am sorry, you had so much pressure on you."

"Hey, darling, it was not your fault, you are home now, and we can enjoy this time together now."

"Yes, very true, so what did Hannah and your parents say when you told them the news?" Chad asks.

"I haven't told anyone else yet, oh well apart from my doctor of course, I wanted you to be the first to know."

"Oh really, that is lovely, hey why don't we invite people over this weekend and tell everyone then?"

"Are you sure you are up to visitors, you just got home?"

"Absolutely, I am so excited, I want to tell everyone."

"Ok then, we will do it" you respond excitedly.

CHAPTER 15

*T*he weekend arrives, and your house is a buzz of excitement, with both yours and Chad's families, Hannah, Trevor and both your and Chad's colleagues from work.

The rouse for the gathering, is to celebrate Chad's birthday and recovery from his accident. As everyone is enjoying the food and festivities, Chad excitedly calls for everyone's attention.

"Hey everyone, can I have your attention?", everyone stops and focuses on Chad.

Chad continues "Thanks everyone, thank you all for being here today with us to celebrate my birthday and my recovery from the accident, it means a lot to me". Chad pulls you in close next to him and continues trying to hide his excitement, "Actually, there is another reason, we invited you all here today, Angela gave me the best birthday present ever this week, We are finally pregnant!!".

The crowd erupts with cheers and rush to engulf you both in a group hug.

Hannah eventually can pull you aside and with a huge smile engulfs you in one of her bear hugs. "Oh Angela, I am so excited, our babies are going to grow up together, you have to tell me all about it, I want all the details".

"Really Hannah, do you want all the details?" you question her with a smile.

"Oh well, maybe not all the details, but how far along are you? When did you find out? And why didn't you tell me first?"

 "Ok, I found about the day of Chad's accident, so I am about eight weeks along so far, and with everything that was going on with Chad, I wanted to tell him first, I am sorry".

"I understand perfectly, so how are you feeling?"

"Yeah, ok, tired and the nausea is a hard".

"Tell me about" replies Hannah, "It was awful, so glad at nearly six months along now, it has settled", Hannah rubs her growing baby bump and smiles at you, "We have to go shopping, this is going to be so great".

Just then both yours and Chad's mum make their way to you, tears in the eyes and arms outstretched.

Your mum crying, splutters "Come here baby, I am so happy" and pulls you in.

"Thank you, Mum, Chad and I are so excited".

Chad's mum eagerly awaits to pull you in for a hug also.

"Oh Angela, this is the best news ever, our first grandchild, we are so happy".

"Thank you, Fran,".

You all return to the crowd who are still so excited about the news.

Hours later, the crowd disperse, and it is just you and Chad left. "Well, that went off well, don't you think" says Chad, "everyone was so happy".

"Yes, it was a great day, I am pretty tired now though".

 "Of course, love, we can watch a bit of tv and then head to bed, Mum and my sister cleaned up everything, so we can just relax now".

The day arrives for your first pregnancy scan, you and Chad make your way to the hospital, Chad is slowly recovering and is getting used to his crutches.

As you wait to be called in for the scan, Chad looks at you excitedly, and says "I can't believe we are going to see our baby today, that is unreal, isn't it?".

"I know, it will make it all seem so real, I mean the sickness is real enough, but seeing our baby for the first time, will be amazing".

"Mr and Mrs Williams, the doctor is ready for you now", the nurse shows you into the doctor's office.

"Good morning, you two, are you both ready to see your baby? "the doctor asks with a smile.

"Absolutely," you both respond.

"Great, just lay on the bed here, and we will get started then".

The doctor moves you top back and places the cold gel on your stomach and then the probe.

As she looks on the screen, you both notice her move a little closer to the screen as if to get a better look.

"Is everything ok doctor?" you ask with concern.

"Yes, Yes, everything is fine, it is just I had to get a better look, I see two babies here!" she responds and looks at you both.

"What, where?" exclaims Chad as he grabs your hand tighter and looks at the doctor and at the screen.

You are in shock, as the doctor shows the outlines on the screen. "See, there is one, and there is the other one right there".

"Oh my god, Chad, look, Twins, oh my, what are we going to do" you say to Chad in a mixture of excitement and a sense of fear.

"We are going to have double the fun, aren't we?" Chad responds smiling.

The rest of the appointment seems to go by in a blur as you are still taken aback by the news, as if understanding, the situation, the doctor writes down all the important information you need to remember, especially now you are having twins.

As you make your way back to the car, you can't help but cry.

"Angela, are you ok?" asks Chad worried,

"I just can't believe we are having twins, we waited so long for this, I am just in shock".

"Yeah, I know, this is huge, but we are in this together, it will be fine" he pulls you in close wipes your tears away and kisses you.

After arriving home, your phone pings with a message from Hannah.

"How did the ultrasound go?"

You respond, "It was a surprise for sure, we are having twins!!"

Minutes go by until Hannah responds, "Shit sorry I am in shock, what! are you sure?"

"Yes, we are sure the doctor confirmed it today, we have the ultrasound picture to prove it, Chad and I are in shock as well, but so happy".

"Oh my god Angela, that is fantastic, I am so excited, wait until I tell Trev, when he gets home from shift, unless Chad has already told him".

"No Chad and I haven't told anyone yet, you are the first, we just got home and are still processing the news to be honest".

"Ok, well congratulations you two, I will catch up with you soon to celebrate, love you X".

"Thank you, love you too Bye X".

CHAPTER 16

*T*he next few weeks are hectic for you as you navigate Chad's intense rehabilitation schedule, assist him with his exercises, trying to be strong and supportive for Chad, despite feeling the intense pregnancy symptoms.

It is time for Chad's daily exercise schedule, you begin to set up, you look around for Chad and notice he is missing, you enter the bedroom and find him still lying in bed.

"Hey darling, ready for your exercise session? I have everything set up in the lounge" you ask Chad encouragingly.

Chad turns to face you, he sighs, "I don't feel like it today".

"Hey, don't be like that, you know you need to do the exercises every day" you reply enthusiastically.

"No, I don't want to today, I am tired and just want to stay in bed", Chad responds and turns over.

Not giving up, you sit next to him on the bed, "Talk to me Darling".

Still facing away from you, Chad responds "I don't know why we are bothering with these exercises, I thought I would be finished with those damn crutches by now".

"I understand love, you are doing really well, you had serious injuries, it is going to take time to fully recover, come on let's do a few exercises now" you reply and excitedly pat Chad on the arm.

"Sorry, love, I know you are trying to help, please don't push me today, I just don't feel like it today, I just want to stay here please" Chad responds with his voice almost quivering.

Sensing his mood, you decide not to push him any further, "Ok, sweetheart, you have worked so hard, I guess one day off won't hurt, but you can't get out of it tomorrow, just rest for now then" you kiss Chad and leave him to rest.

"Thanks" replies Chad as he pulls the covers up and snuggles in.

"No worries, let me know if you need anything" you say as you leave the room.

You spend the next several hours, attending to household chores and attending to work assignments. As you put the finishing touches on your last office task, you hear Chad making his way down the hall with his crutches. As he approaches the doorway, you look up, "Hey sweetheart, you are up, how are you feeling now?" you ask.

Chad smiles, "Hey, I am feeling a bit better now, sorry about this morning, just wasn't in the mood for exercises today".

"No worries, glad you are feeling better now, Are you hungry? Do you want some lunch?" you ask.

"Yeah, I guess I could go for a sandwich" Chad replies with a smile.

The next day, you try again to encourage Chad to perform his exercises. "Hey Sweetie, come on, we have to do those exercise today, you can't get out of them today".

Chad grimaces, "Ok, let's get them over with".

"Good lets go then" you say as you begin to set up for the exercises.

You encourage Chad to stretch and extend his leg and shoulder and can see the struggle on his face.

"Come on Darling, you are doing great, nearly there, keep going" you say encouragingly.

"Ah, I am trying, it is so hard and still hurts" Chad replies.

"I know, just one more set, and then you can rest ok".

After the last set, Chad falls into the chair, shaking.

"Great Job, Darling, that will do for now" you hug Chad.

CHAPTER 17

As you lay in bed the next morning, your alarm rings out, you are due to head in for your required to return to the office to attend an important department meeting. You feel so tired and drained, but you quietly drag yourself out of the bed so as not to disturb Chad and head to the bathroom to begin to prepare for the day. As you make your way to the kitchen, you notice Chad is up.

"Good morning sweetheart how are you today?" he asks bright and cheerily.

"Morning, you are up?" you bluntly respond.

Chad looks over at you, "Are you ok sweetie?"

"No not really, I feel crap", you respond grumpily.

"Oh, that is not good, have some breakfast, that might help".

"No, I don't feel that I can stomach anything at the moment".

Still trying to be bright, Chad responds, "You have to eat something, perhaps some dry toast, I heard that might help with morning sickness", he makes his way to the pantry with his crutches.

"No Chad, I really don't want anything" you snap as you slump into the stool at the kitchen bench.

 "Ok, no worries, just trying to help" says Chad a little deflated.

You both sit in silence for a little while until you are ready to leave to head to work. As you grab your work items and head out the door, you give Chad a quick kiss on the cheek, sigh and head out the door.

Chad calls after you, "Bye sweetie, have a good day".

As you get in your car, you feel guilt over being grumpy with Chad, but you cannot help feeling unwell, you sigh, and hope you will feel better by the time you get to work and make a promise to yourself to make it up to Chad when you get home.

A little while later, you arrive at work, and the nausea you were feeling earlier has subsided a bit, and you begin to feel better. It is the first day back in the office since you and Chad announced your pregnancy and discovered that you were now expecting twins, as you arrive at your office you are met with the most amazing sight as you reach the door of your office. Your office has been completely decorated with pink and blue streamers, balloons, confetti, and stuffed baby toys. You cannot help but shriek with excitement, and tears roll down your face, as you turn around, your office colleagues are there smiling with arms outstretched for hugs and well wishes.

Finally, you are able to respond, "Thank you everyone, this is amazing and so unexpected", tears still rolling down your face.

Greta makes her way to you, gives you a big hug, "Angela, we are all so happy for you and we wanted to celebrate again with you".

"Thank you, Greta, this is beautiful".

After spending some time talking to your fellow colleagues, you decide to get to work and prepare for the meeting scheduled for just after lunch, you remember to take photos of the decorations to show Chad when you get home, you clear the lovely pink and blue teddy bear shaped confetti from your desk and settle in for the day ahead.

The rest of the morning passes by and as you were unable to face breakfast this morning, your stomach begins to growl alerting to you to lunch time.

Feeling better in the stomach now, you make your way to the office cafeteria for lunch. You choose some sandwiches and fruit and find a quiet table in the sun outside. Shortly after sitting down, a familiar face appears, it is Derrick, "Hey Angela, do you mind if I join you?"

"Hey Derrick, for sure, take a seat" you respond gesturing for him to take the spare seat at the table in front of you.

"So, Angela, congratulations on your pregnancy, I am so excited for you and Chad, I know how much you wanted a baby"

"Thanks Derrick, yes Chad and I are so excited".

"So how have you been? And how is Chad's recovery going? it was such a shock to hear about his accident".

"Thanks Derrick, yes, I am going ok, the morning sickness is a bit hard, but getting through it, Chad is coming a long really well with his recovery, he still has a little while left on his crutches, but he is doing well with his physiotherapy treatments, so we are hoping he can go back to work in about 4-6 weeks".

"Oh, wow that is good news, "

You both continue to eat your lunches, "Derrick, how are you and Bree doing?"

You sense Derrick tense up a little, "We are Ok I guess" he responds but avoids your eye contact.

"Oh, what is going on? Do you want to talk about it?"

"I don't want to trouble you with my problems" responds Derrick.

"Derrick, if I am honest, what with pregnancy hormones and Chad's accident, I would appreciate the distraction. Besides we are mates, aren't we? I would love to help if I can".

"Thanks Angela, I could use a mate at the moment, a female perspective if you like,"

"Ok, go ahead" you focus on Derrick.

Derrick continues, "Since I found out about your pregnancy, I was really excited, so I thought it would be a good time to broach the subject with Bree again, so on the weekend, I planned a nice little day trip and a picnic".

"Oh, that sounds lovely" you gently interrupt.

"Yes, I thought so" continues Derrick, "Anyway, while we were having lunch, I told Bree about your news, and how excited I was for you and then I suggested that we should try for our own baby, well, that went down like a lead balloon actually".

"Oh, Derrick that is not good, what happened?" you ask.

"Well, Bree got all quiet at first and when I tried to get her to talk, she flipped out and basically told me she was beginning to come to the realisation that she may not ever want to have a baby at all" Derrick face fills with sadness.

"Oh Derrick, that is awful, are you sure that is how she really feels? maybe she was just surprised" you ask trying to be reassuring.

"I think she is serious, she told me how much she is loving her new role and she is not prepared to sacrifice all she has worked for to get this far in her role. She actually accused me of being selfish, expecting her to give up her work to have a baby".

"Derrick I am sorry, what happened next?"

"We got into a bit of an argument, and she started to pack up the picnic and demanded that we go home straight away, which we did, and things have been very strained ever since, neither of us are game to broach the subject again, as we don't want to start another argument, so we have been walking on eggshells around each other"

"Just give it a bit more time, perhaps you both need a little longer to calm down and see each other's side".

"Maybe you are right Angela, any idea of how long I should wait, and what I should do in the meantime?" Derrick asks hopefully.

"Oh well, let me see", you stop and think for a bit and then continue, "Well I can see both sides of the situation, Bree has worked hard to get where she has in her firm, I can understand that she may feel that if she was to have a baby now, she could lose all she has worked for, perhaps you could see if you could both sit down and discuss some options, like for example, instead of Bree having to take full maternity leave, could you both perhaps share it a little, do you think you could take time off and be a stay at home Dad for a while? Or could you afford a nanny?"

"They are good ideas Angela, I just don't know if Bree is willing to talk about it, she got really angry on the weekend".

"Well, all I can suggest is that you give it a try, spoil her with a nice dinner, make sure you tell her how proud you are of her achievements at work and how you would be willing to look into alternatives, if she was willing to meet you halfway through".

"Thanks Angela, I will give it some more thought, and try again soon" Derrick responds, and a smile appears on his face. "So back to you, how are the baby plans progressing?"

"Well, I haven't told anyone else here at work, but Chad and I found out last week that we are actually expecting twins".

Derrick face lights up, "Oh my that is huge news, congratulations, you must be both so excited".

"Yes, we are, it is still sinking in to be honest, and I am trying not to freak out, I know I desperately wanted a baby, but two at once is another thing entirely."

"I am sure it would be messing with you mind, but it is fantastic news, you will be a natural I am sure".

"Oh, Derrick I hope so, the mood swings are kicking in a bit, I was pretty grumpy with poor Chad this morning".

"Oh, he will understand".

"Oh, I hope so".

You both sit for a bit longer before realising that lunch time is over and you both head back to work and you head to the boardroom and join your fellow colleagues.

Rick and Greta enter the room and call everyone's attention. As the room falls silent, Rick begins "Good afternoon everyone, thanks for joining us today, I am pleased to advise we will be merging with competing advertising agency Carpenter Media. The merger will be taking effect on July 1, so in approx. 4 months."

You and your fellow colleagues are both surprised and excited.

Greta stands up to address the group, "I am sure you will all have a lot of questions, please rest assured that all jobs are safe. Carpenter Media has a large customer base, so there will be an increase in workload for everyone and an increase in variety of clientele, so exciting times ahead, we will need all hands-on deck to ensure this merger is seamless and effective".

Rick then takes over, "The managers of Carpenter Media will be joining us next week to meet everyone and gain a feel for our operations. I will now show you a powerpoint presentation of Carpenter Media and their business structure."

After watching the presentation, Rick says "This is an exciting move for us, If you have any questions, please do not hesitate to come and see either Greta or myself, Thanks everyone, that is all for now".

As you return to your office to take in the news from the meeting your colleague Stacey joins you to discuss the meeting. "So, Angela what do you think of the merger?" Stacey asks.

"Well, sounds like it should be a great idea, from what I have heard of Carpenter Media, they have some pretty high-profile clients. So, it will be an interesting new line of business for us".

"Yes, it will be exciting to have new ideas and expand our business" Stacey responds with a smile.

"Yes, exciting times for sure" you say.

Stacey heads back to her office and you begin to focus on your projects for the remainder of the day and as 5.00pm comes, you eagerly pack up and head home to see Chad, you still feel guilty for this morning.

As you arrive home, you enter to find Chad sleeping on the couch, he looks so peaceful, as you approach him, you wonder should I wake him? The urge to wake him is too hard to resist, you kneel on the floor next to him and place a passionate kiss on his lips. He initially jumps and then realising what is happening, he wraps you in his arms and pulls you onto the couch with him. You straddle him, continuing the kiss. Eventually, you pull away smiling, "Welcome home sweetheart, this is a lovely wake up" Chad whispers catching his breath.

"Hello, my darling, I missed you" you respond as you lower in for another kiss.

"Glad you are feeling better than this morning" Chad replies smiling as he strokes your hair as he holds you tightly.

"Yes, I am feeling better, sorry about being snappy this morning".

"That's Ok, I understand" replies Chad sweetly.

You both continue to lay in each other's arms for a while longer as you both discuss your days respectively. Chad is exciting to hear the news about the new company merger. "Wow sounds like a great thing for the company, new clients will be great for growth" Chad says.

"Yes definitely, it is really exciting, How was your day sweetheart?" you ask.

"It has been good; I have been busy focusing on my physio exercises and catching up on some paperwork that Wally had sent over from the firehouse".

"Oh, that is good sweetheart".

You begin to tell Chad about the wonderful surprise that awaited you at the office when you arrived and show him the photos of how your office was decorated.

"Oh, that is wonderful of them" he smiles as he flicks through the photos on your phone. "Did you tell them the news that we were having twins?" he asked excitedly.

"No, I only told Derrick when we were having lunch together, He was so thrilled for us".

"Oh, you had lunch with Derrick?" Chad asks, you sense him tensing up.

"Yes, he happened to be in the cafeteria when I stopped by for lunch today, and we had our lunches together and caught up."

"Oh, I see" says Chad.

You can sense concern from Chad. "Are you Ok Chad?"

"Yes, I am just surprised that you only decided to tell Derrick about our news, I would be yelling it from the rooftops, in fact I have already told Wally when he popped over earlier".

"Oh great, what did Wally say?"

"He was so excited for us"

"I was just overwhelmed I guess by the fuss of the decorations, and then by the time I composed myself and settled in for the day, I got busy, and then the meeting   and I was distracted, I am still in shock I guess about the whole thing, having twins is huge, I will tell them next week when I go back into the office".

"Ok, sounds good, I guess we better look at organising something for dinner then" Chad responds.

You sense the change of subject, and can't help but question Chad, "You're not jealous of Derrick, are you? He is just a mate from work, that is all".

"No, I am not jealous, I was just surprised to hear that you had lunch with him is all, Now let's get up an organise dinner, you must be hungry, I know I am getting peckish" replies Chad as he makes a move for his crutches to head to the kitchen. You still feel a little concerned by Chad's reaction to Derrick, but you decide to let it go, and follow him into the kitchen. Considering his reaction to

Derrick, you decide not to discuss the issues that Derrick and Bree are having with regards to having a baby.

CHAPTER 18

*T*he next night you arrange to catch up with Hannah, she is approaching her seventh month of her pregnancy and you soon will need to organise her baby shower. You both meet at Giuseppe's and enjoy dinner while you share ideas for the shower. You have been collecting ideas for the last couple of months and are now ready to finalise the plans.

Hannah has decided to have the shower at her house in the backyard, so you begin to talk about decorations and food.

"So, Hannah, what type of food do you want to have?" you ask with pen and paper in hand to finalise details.

 "I am thinking about finger foods, like sandwiches, little pies and quiches etc, oh, there is an awesome little bakery near my house that can cater for it, they only need two weeks' notice to prepare everything. We need to have little pink and blue cupcakes as well." replies Hannah excitedly.

"That sounds great, I will go and see them tomorrow and work out what they can organise" you reply as you excitedly write down the list. "Now what about decorations?"

Hannah thinks momentarily, then says "Naturally we will have to have balloons, pink and blue of course"

"Streamers, you have to have streamers, bows and little teddy bears,"

"Oh, that sounds awesome, love it" smiles Hannah, as you add these items to the ever growing to do list.

"Can you think of any games to play at the party?" you ask Hannah.

You both stop and think.

Hannah replies "I have heard of a game called "Who is that Baby?" where the guests bring a baby photo of themselves, and we all have to guess who the baby photo belongs to".

"Sounds great," you add, I have also heard of Guess the baby food game, where different kinds of baby food are placed in unlabelled jars and then we have to guess what the food is,"

 "Ok, good one, replies Hannah, "there is also a How many baby items can you name game, where the person who lists the greatest number of baby items in two minutes wins a prize".

"Ooh like it, we can also do diaper changing relay race" you add,

You both laugh, "Yes, they sound good, I think that will do for games for now., I think that is it, we have covered food, decorations, and games, we have done well", you say to Hannah smiling "Excellent, I will get the invitations out this week, and the party is all set for four weeks from this Saturday, how exciting".

"Yes, can't wait, thank you so much Angela, it will be fantastic" says Hannah giving you a big hug.

You both spend the next hour enjoying dessert and catching up on each other's news.

"So, Angela, how is the pregnancy going for you?" asks Hannah.

You sit back in your chair, gently rubbing your stomach, your baby bump is starting to show now. You sigh and respond, "Well so far it is going alright. I get very tired and wow the morning sickness and mood swings are bit extreme at times".

"That all sounds normal to me" replies Hannah, "I was tired to begin with too, that eased in the 2nd trimester, but now that I am well into the 3rd trimester, I am feeling wiped out again. Oh, and don't get me started on the mood swings, poor Trev, didn't know what he was going to face each time he got home. He was an angel about it though".

"Yes, poor Chad, I snapped at him the other morning, when he tried to make me breakfast before work, poor guy" you say with a smile.

"Chad will understand, plus you are having twins, so the emotions will be heightened for sure" reassures Hannah.

"Yes, Chad has been so good".

You both finish up your catch up, pay your bill and head home. Chad is waiting up for you as you return home, "Hi Honey, how was your dinner with Hannah?" Chad asks as he pulls you down next to him on the couch, holding your tight and planting a kiss on your lips.

"It was really lovely, we set all the plans for her baby shower in a months' time".

"Oh, that is good news" replies Chad.

"Yes, we planned the food, entertainment and decorations so, I will get the invitations out in the next couple of days, and order the food etc", you respond with a yawn.

"Sounds like a busy night, you must be tired, let's get ready to head to bed" Chad says.

"Yeah, I am pretty tired" you smile and start to rub your small baby bump.

Chad responds by placing his hand on yours and caresses your bump, "It is all real now, isn't it? now we can see these beautiful babies growing".

"Yes, I am excited that it I am now beginning to show" you respond smiling while looking at your baby bump.

CHAPTER 19

A month later you wake up and the familiar feeling of nausea is overwhelming, as you lie still trying to not to move hoping the feeling will pass, you think to yourself" Gee, how long before this morning sickness ends". You place your hand gently on your growing bump, you are soon entering your second trimester. Just as your mind begins to wander to thoughts of your babies, the bedroom door opens, and Chad is standing there smiling. "Good morning sweetheart, how did you sleep? Are you ready for breakfast? He inquires as he makes his way over to the bed and leans down to plant a kiss on your lips.

You jump out of the bed and race to the bathroom just in time before emptying the contents of your stomach. Chad rushes after you, helping to hold your hair back and rubbing your back, he asks "Darling, are you Ok?"

"No, I am not!" you can't help but snap back before vomiting again.

"Oh sweetheart, is there anything I can do?" Chad asks.

"No there isn't" you respond as you fall to floor, tears welling up in your eyes.

Chad reaches for a face washer, wets it and hands it to you to wipe your face and freshen up. "Oh sweetie, this morning sickness is still going on, thought it would be easing by this stage" he questions as he caresses your hair.

"Yeah, well obviously it is not over with yet" you respond as you wipe your face. "I think it is settling down for now, but I just want to go back to bed for a bit and just lay still".

As you make your way back to bed, Chad follows you "Yes of course sweetheart, is there anything I can get for you?"

"No, I just want to lay here" you say trying to smile.

"No worries," Chad says as he helps you back into bed, "you rest for a while, we have the appointment with my specialist later today, I will get you up later on".

Still feeling weak, you respond "What?"

"I have the appointment with the specialist this afternoon, I should be able to find out if I can go back to work soon, remember?"

Placing your hands on your face "Oh no, I forgot about that, what time is the appointment again?"

"It is at 1.30pm, we will need to leave by 12pm to head there".

"Oh no, hopefully I will feel better after a bit more of a sleep".

"Sorry sweetheart, I feel bad that you feel so sick and have to take me" says Chad, he pauses for a moment, and then smiles, "I will call Trevor and see if he can take me, so you can stay here and rest".

"Really, is that possible?"

"Maybe, he is not rostered on today, I will call him and see if he is free".

"That would be wonderful if he could, I just feel pretty bad today, and just want to stay here".

"Of course, I will call him now and let you know, you just rest" says Chad as he caresses your hair and he plants a kiss on your forehead, and then leaves the room.

A little while later as you are just about to drift off to sleep, Chad comes back into the room, making his way to the bed. "Hey, sorry to wake you, I just spoke to Trevor, he is fine to take me to the appointment later. Hannah will come over with him and stay with you while we are gone". You smile at Chad, "Thanks sweetheart, I really appreciate it, Sorry I can't take you today, Hannah and I can check on the final plans for the baby shower this weekend too".

"No worries, just rest now, let me know if you need anything".

You nod your head smiling and close your eyes to return to sleep before Hannah arrives later.

After a short sleep you awaken and although still feeling a little weak, you are relieved to feel that the nausea appears to have passed for today and begin to feel a little bit hungry.

You decide to get up and make your way to kitchen to check on Chad. As you make your way to the kitchen you remember that you have some left-over chocolate from yesterday, you begin to search the pantry unable to find the chocolate. Just as you are searching the shelves, Chad comes into the kitchen. "Hey sweetheart, you are up, how are you feeling now?" he asks.

"I am trying to find that chocolate bar I left in here yesterday, do you know where it is?" you ask as you continue to move everything in the pantry.

"Oh yeah, sorry I finished that off earlier".

"What no, I really wanted it, what am I going to eat now" you respond, emotions take over and you feel yourself tearing up.

"Oh sweetheart, I am sorry, didn't know you wanted it, I can make you something else if you want, do you want some eggs or toast?" Chad asks.

"No, I wanted the chocolate bar" you respond, and you feel your emotions take over and burst into tears.

Chad pulls you in close, "Sorry sweetheart, don't cry, I will get some more when I go out later ok".

"Thanks, that would be great" you say still in Chad's embrace. "Sorry for getting so upset about the chocolate, these hormones are hard to handle sometimes".

"It's ok, honey, I understand" Chad says smiling.

"Thanks for understanding, I feel really silly though" you say as you pull away and wipe the tears from your eyes. "I think I will go and have a shower to freshen up before Hannah and Trevor arrives".

"Ok, sounds good, enjoy".

The shower refreshes you and you feel better, as you exit the bedroom, the doorbell rings. Hannah and Trevor have arrived. Hannah rushes forward to give you a big bear hug, "How are you feeling? Chad said you were pretty sick this morning?" Hannah asks.

"Yeah, I am feeling a bit better now, still having pretty intense morning sickness, and don't get me started on the mood swings" you respond raising your eyebrows in exasperation.

 "Oh yeah, the mood swings, poor Trev, he copped some pretty intense episodes" Hannah laughs and slaps Trevor on the arm in jest.

"Oh yeah, I never knew what I was going to face when I returned home" replies Trevor laughing.

"Hey buddy, thanks for coming and taking me to the appointment today" says Chad, shaking Trevor's hand and pulling him for a man hug.

"All good buddy are you ready to go then?" asks Trevor.

"Yes, I will just grab my jacket and we can leave".

Chad goes to the closet and grabs his jacket, he gives you a hug and kiss and follows Trevor to the front door, he turns around and says "Hannah, thank you so much for coming over and staying with Angela, she was quite sick this morning, I am glad she won't be alone".

"No worries Chad, my pleasure, we can have a good girly catchup" replies Hannah and gives Chad a hug. "Good luck at the specialist"

You spend the next couple of hours relaxing with Hannah, discussing the final plans for the baby shower on Saturday as well as the fact that Hannah is only a month away from giving birth, she is both nervous and excited.

A little while later, Chad and Trevor return home.

"Hey ladies, how was your afternoon?" asks Chad as he enters the room, making his way over to you and gives you a kiss.

Trevor follows behind, pulling Hannah in for a kiss "Hey baby," he says.

"We had a great catch up, finalised all the plans for Saturday, How did your appointment go?" you ask.

"Really good, the doctor is really impressed with my recovery and the reports from the physiotherapist, so he has given me all clear to return to work at the end of next week" Chad says smiling.

"Oh, that is great news, so excited for you sweetheart" you reply and plant a kiss on Chad's lips.

"Chad, that is great news, congratulations" says Hannah and hugs Chad.

"Yes, I am so relieved to be getting back to normal now, well at least normal until the babies arrive" replies Chad giving you a wink. "Oh sweetheart, I nearly forgot, look what I picked up for you on the way home", Chad hands you a small brown bag. You open the bag and peek inside to find six new chocolate bars. "Oh sweetie, thank you" you say smiling to Chad.

CHAPTER 20

*T*he rest of the week flies by and the day of Hannah's baby shower arrives. As you wake up, you are relieved to find that the morning sickness seems to be staying away for the day and your emotions are behaving, you tell yourself, "Oh that is a relief, I am feeling good today". You and Chad get ready to head over to Hannah and Trevor's. The boys have decided to have their own celebration and head out for a day of golf.

As you both arrive, Chad helps Trevor set up the tables and seating for the party and then they get ready to head off for their day of fun.

"Hey ladies, do you need anything else before we head off?" asks Trevor.

"No sweetheart, all good, thanks, you go and have a great day, our guests will be arriving soon" says Hannah.

"Ok, great, you two have a great time, everything looks fantastic, you have both done so well." Says Trevor hugging both you and Hannah.

Chad pulls you in for a farewell kiss and hug, "You have done a fantastic job sweetheart, have a great day".

With that, Chad and Trevor head out and you and Hannah continue setting up the food and decorations ready for the party.

As you finish setting up, you both stand back, look at each other and smile with relief. "Looks amazing Angela, thank so much for all your help."

"It does look good, doesn't it? it was my pleasure to help".

You both hug each other, you both have time for refreshing drink of non-alcoholic punch. Just as you take a sip of your drink, the doorbell rings signalling the first of the guests arrive.

"I'll get it" you say as you make your way to the door.

The first guest to arrive in Hannah's mother, Wendy.

"Hello Wendy, welcome, come in".

"Hello Angela, how are you darling? great to see you".

Wendy follows you through to the kitchen, where Hannah is putting the finishing touches on the cupcake platter.

"Hi Mum, so glad you are here" Hannah says excitedly, and she races towards her mum and pulls her in for a big hug.

"Hi Darling, this looks fantastic, you and Angela have done a fantastic job. Is there anything I can do to help you?"

"No Mum, we are pretty much done now, just sit down, have a drink of punch and relax."

The rest of the guests start to arrive, and the house is a hive of activity, with everyone excitedly gathering around Hannah, enjoying the delicious foods and drinks on offer.

The time has arrived for Hannah to begin to open the gifts that everyone has generously brought. Hannah makes her way to the table which is stacked full. As she starts to open the first gift, she places her hand on her stomach and smiles, "Oh wow, baby is excited for all these wonderful presents, he or she is kicking excitedly".

Everyone laughs and claps.

As Hannah finishes opening the last present, she looks at the wonderful presents and tears of happiness form in her eyes. "Thank you everyone, this has been amazing, Trev, baby and I are so thankful for all these wonderful gifts".

Everyone claps and smiles, forming a line to hug Hannah.

You look at the display of opened gifts and see a variety of beautiful baby outfits, toys, nappies, vouchers, baby care items, you can't help but take mental notes of all the items that you and Chad will need in approximately five months.

The rest of the afternoon goes by so fast; the house is filled with laughter as everyone joins in the games. As the guests begin to leave, everyone is smiling and happy with the day as a whole.

After the last guest leaves, Hannah turns to you, and smiles, she pulls you in for a hug. "This was a great day, Angela, thanks again."

"Oh, I am so happy you have had a great day, everyone was so happy".

Just then, the door opens and Chad and Trevor return from their day of golf.

"Hey ladies, how did everything go? Wow looks at all the fantastic presents" says Trevor as he hugs Hannah and heads towards the present table perusing all the gifts.

"Hi Honey, it was a fantastic day, yes everyone was so generous, How was your day boys?" say Hannah.

"We had a great day, I beat Trev at golf, we met up with a couple of the guys from the firehouse," smiles Chad as he plants a kiss on your lips and pulls you in close.

You and Chad help Hannah and Trevor clean up and then feeling tired you leave and head home.

On the drive home, you turn to Chad, "Today was such a great day, everyone was so generous, it is amazing how much stuff you need for a baby, and we have two, so we will need so much more stuff".

"Yes, it's amazing how much stuff babies need, we will have to start preparing now hey?"

"Yes, very true, at least after today, I got heaps of ideas of what we will need."

As you arrive home, you settle down in front of the television and have a snack for dinner and head off to bed early as it has been such a big day.

Several days later, Chad awakens you from your deep sleep with a passionate kiss.

"Happy Anniversary Sweetheart"

"Yes, Happy Anniversary Darling" you respond smiling and stretching awake.

"When you are ready, I have a big day planned for us sweetheart" Chad says excitedly as he pulls you close.

"Oh, really, that sounds exciting, what are we doing?"

"Well, firstly, I have a nutritious yummy breakfast planned, then we get to see our growing babies again today at the next ultrasound, then we will go shopping and start gathering all that we will need for their arrival. Then to finish off our day, I have dinner booked for us at your favourite restaurant".

"Oh Chad, that sounds fantastic, I can't wait."

"Excellent, but first let's have some fun before we get up for breakfast" Chad says as he kisses you passionately and caresses your breasts and growing baby bump.

"That sounds great" you respond, pulling him close with a passionate kiss.

As you both release into the passion of pleasuring each other, you lay next to each other catching your breath.

You both shower and enjoy your breakfast of muesli scrambled eggs and toast.

Before you know it, it is time to get ready to head to your ultrasound appointment. As you enter the hospital, you squeeze Chad's hand tightly. Feelings of both nervousness and excitement begin to rise inside you.

Chad looks at you and asks with concern, "Are you ok sweetie?"

"Yes, of course, I am just excited to see our babies and anxious to make sure that everything is ok." you reply with a nervous smile.

"I know Darling, I feel the same way, everything will be fine".

You check in at the reception desk and take your seats in the waiting room. The minutes seem to take hours to pass before your name is called. You enter the room and prepare for the ultrasound.

The doctor enters smiling, "Hi Angela and Chad, how are you both today? Ready to see your babies?"

You respond, "Hi doctor, we are great and so ready to see our babies".

Chad grabs your hand "Yes Doctor, we can't wait "

"Ok, let's get started, are you ready Angela, I am about to place the gel now, it will be cold".

You nod smiling "All ready doctor".

You and Chad focus on the screen and hold your breath as your babies appear on the screen,

As the examination continues, the doctor advises that everything is looking good, the babies are growing as expected. "Now, would you like to know the genders of your babies?" the doctor asks.

You and Chad look at each other and after a minute's thought, you turn to the doctor smiling, "No, we think we want to wait".

"Not a problem, it will be exciting to find out in a few short months, Now Angela, how is everything going? Are you still having morning sickness episodes?

"No Doctor, everything is going quite well at the moment, the morning sickness appears to have settled for now, which is a relief" you respond.

Chad chimes in with a laugh "Yes, I have noticed her mood swings are improving too". You playfully slap Chad on the arm smiling.

"Very good, that is great to hear, well everything looks wonderful at the moment, keep doing what you are doing, and we will see you again in a month's time for the next checkup, unless you need anything before then, don't hesitate to contact me, I will have my assistant make another appointment for you and give you a copy of the ultrasound to take home, Also have you considered joining a birthing class, we have one scheduled to start in a couple of weeks."

"No, I hadn't thought about that, that sounds good," you respond looking at Chad.

"Yes, they can be very helpful to learn about labour, the birthing process and preparing for the baby, and considering that you are having twins, I highly recommend you attend the class, I will have my assistant sign you up for the next class."

"Great, thanks doctor" you say as you get dressed.

As you return to the car, the nerves you felt earlier begin to disappear, you and Chad both look longingly at the ultrasound pictures.

"Wow, they are amazing aren't they sweetheart?" says Chad.

"Yes, I am so relieved that they are growing so well".

"I can't believe we are going back to school with these classes" laughs Chad.

"Yes, I know, we will have to pay attention, been a while since we were in school" you respond laughing.

You both spend the rest of the afternoon, walking around the local baby supplies store. The sales assistant is very knowledgeable and creates a detailed list for you both, from cribs, prams, nursery supplies and clothing. With only a few months to go, you place orders for the nursery furniture and cribs.

You both head home excited and relieved that you have begun to prepare the nursery for your babies and begin to prepare for your anniversary dinner.

As you arrive at the restaurant, the maître d, welcomes you and shows you to a secluded table decorated with romantic flowers and candles.

"Oh Chad, this is gorgeous, thank you".

"My pleasure sweetheart" Chad smiles as he helps you to your seat.

As he sits, he pours you both a non-alcoholic cider. He raises his glass to your, "Happy anniversary sweetheart, this year has been amazing, and I am so excited to meet our new babies, you have made me the happiest man alive".

You raise your glass to Chad, and respond "Darling, I am so happy and excited for the year we have had, and for the future, I love you so much."

Chad leans in and kisses you.

You enjoy your meal and dessert, followed by a romantic dance on the dancefloor, Chad pulls you in close as you both sway to the music.

As you make your way home, you feel so happy, you have both had an amazing day. Just as you settle into bed for the evening, you feel a strange sensation in your stomach, which makes you jump, "Oh wow, I think the babies just kicked" you exclaim. Chad rushes to your side and places his hand on your stomach, "Wow really let me feel".

Just then the babies move again, Chad jumps in surprise, tears start to form in his eyes "Oh my that is amazing".

As you settle in the bed for the night, you both keep your hands on your stomach, enjoying the babies' active movements for the next few minutes until you all fall asleep after the big, exciting day you have had.

CHAPTER 21

*L*ater that week, Chad is ready to return to work, it has been approximately ten weeks since his accident and he is fully recovered. His team are excited to have him back. He kisses you goodbye as he heads off to work.

"Good luck sweetheart, have a safe shift".

"Thanks sweetie, I am excited to get back to it, I have missed it".

You watch him leave and then prepare for your day at work. You arrive at work intime for the weekly management meeting. The new account you all have been working on for the last few months has been a huge success and your client is requesting a new pitch for a new product line. You spend the rest of the day, brainstorming potential pitch ideas, you commit to potentially three ideas to present to the client at the end of the week.

As you make your way back to the office, you pass Derek's office, you poke your head around the door and find him studying his screen.

"Hey buddy, you look deep in thought, how are things going" you ask, breaking his stare.

"Hey Angela, yes I am stuck on a programming problem, how are you going?"

"Doing really well thanks, just finished the long meeting to plan for the new pitch for the Anderson Group account, it's lunchtime, do you want to grab some lunch at the cafeteria?" you ask Derrick.

Derrick smiles, and replies, "That sounds like a great idea, I could definitely use a break, let's go".

You both make your way to the cafeteria and make your selections and take a seat.

"So, Angela it has been a while since we have caught up, how are things going? How is Chad going?" Derrick asks.

"Yes, it has been a while hasn't it, Chad is doing so well, he is fully recovered now, it is actually his first day back on shift today?"

"Oh, that is great news, he must have been going stir crazy at home I bet".

"Yes, absolutely, he definitely missed the action of his call outs and working with his team, so how are you and Bree going?"

Derrick's face lights up "Bree is doing really well, as you suggested some time back, we had a really good chat about having a baby, and she remained calm, and was willing to listen to my side instead of shutting me down".

"Derrick that is good news, did it work?"

"Yes, actually, it did, she was happy to hear that I would be willing to work from home to jointly care for a baby, so she is more open to the idea of having a baby, now that she knows that all the workload wouldn't fall on her shoulders, so you could say that we are officially trying for a baby now" says Derrick excitedly.

"Excellent Derrick, I am so happy for you, that is great news,"

"So how are things going with your pregnancy Angela, everything going ok?

"Yes, the babies are growing really well, we had an ultrasound last week and the doctor is really happy with how the babies are growing."

"Excellent Angela, did you decide to find out the gender of your twins?"

"No, Chad and I have decided not to find out the genders until they are born."

"I respect that, life has few surprises nowadays" says Derrick.

You both spend the rest of your lunch break catching up and then head back to work for the remainder of your day.

At the end of the day, you make your way home, prepare a quick easy meal for one as Chad is still on shift, watch a bit of television and get ready to head to bed. Just as you get comfortable in bed and begin to drift off to sleep, your phone rings, you think aloud, "Who can that be at this time of night?"

"Hello?" you ask.

"Angela, help, I think the baby is coming now!" you hear coming down the phone line.

"Hannah is that you? Are you ok?" you reply.

"Yes, it's Hannah, Angela, I need you now, the baby is coming now, please come now".

"Ok lovely, calm down, I will be right there, have you tried to call Trev?"

Hannah screams back at you "Yes, I have tried to call him, but he is not answering, Aaaghh, another contraction is coming now, Ouch".

"OK, I am on my way, just try and relax".

"Hurry Angela, I need you I am scared" Hannah screams sobbing.

You jump out of bed, get dressed and race to Hannah. As you in the car, you try to call Chad, but he doesn't answer, "Great they must be on a call" you decide to leave a message "Chad, call me when you can, Hannah is in labour, I am going to take her to the hospital, love you".

Hannah meets you at the door crying and holding her stomach. "Thank goodness you are here, the baby is early, I am scared Angela".

You hold Hannah, "It's going to be ok, let's get you to the hospital, you grab her hospital bag and help her to the car and shortly after you arrive at the hospital. The nurse leads Hannah to the hospital room and eases her onto the bed.

Shortly, the doctor comes in and examines Hannah,

"Well Hannah, you will be here for a while, you only dilated three centimetres, just relax" says the Doctor.

"Thanks Doc, easier said than done" exclaims Hannah.

"I understand you are anxious, but it is best to try and relax as much as you can, is your husband here yet?" asks the doctor.

"Oh, we are not married yet, but no he is at work, I can't reach him he is a firefighter and is on shift" replies Hannah.

"Oh, ok, as I said there is plenty of time" the doctor says and turns to you, and whispers "Good that you are here to keep her calm."

"Yes, I will do my best" you reply.

"Great, Hannah, I will come back and check on you in a little while, if you need anything please press the buzzer" says the doctor as he turns to leave.

"Thanks Doc" you and Hannah respond in unison.

"Oh no another contraction is coming" says Hannah as she grabs your hand.

"Breathe through it Hannah, you got this," you reply soothingly as you stroke her hand.

As the contraction ends, and Hannah regains her breath she looks at you, "Thank you Angela, I don't know what I would do without you here, Can you try and call Chad or Trev again please?"

"Of course, love" you say as you reach for your phone and dial Chad, it reverts to message bank again, you leave Chad another message "Hi honey, can you call me as soon as you can, Hannah is in labour, and we are at the hospital. Love you".

"Sorry Hannah, still message bank, they must be out on a call, do you want to try and watch some TV for a bit?" you ask Hannah.

"Yes Ok," Hannah replies.

You spend the next couple of hours watching late night TV until the doctor returns to check in on Hannah,

"Good news, you are progressing well, you are now approx. six centimetres dilated now, you are doing a great job".

"Thanks Doc,

"Great, I will come back in a little while to check on you again" says the doctor, as he turns to leave, Trevor rushes through the door almost crashing into the doctor.

"Oh Hannah, Are you alright, I am here now, sorry we were on a job" says Trevor almost breathless as he rushes to Hannah's side grabbing her hand.

The doctor turns to Trevor, "Are you the father?"

"Yes doctor, I am Trevor, are Hannah and the baby, ok?" replies Trevor shaking the doctor's hand.

"Yes, she is doing a great job, she is progressing well, but she still has a little way to go, I will leave you two alone and will be back in a little while to check on the progress." says the doctor as he turns to leave the room.

"Trev, I am so glad you are here now, I am so scared, the baby is early" Hannah says crying.

"It will be alright, I am here now" says Trevor as he places a kiss on Hannah's lips,

Just then another contraction hits and Hannah grabs Trevor's hand and cries out.

"It's alright Darling, breathe, I am here now" says Trevor as he strokes Hannah forehead.

You turn to Chad, "Thank goodness you are here, let's go outside and leave these two alone".

"Yes, good idea" Chad responds,

"Hannah and Trevor, we will leave you two alone, we will just be in the waiting room if you need anything" you say as you squeeze Hannah's shoulder and give her and Trevor each a kiss on the cheek.

"Thanks Angela, Thanks for everything you have done so far" Hannah responds.

"My pleasure love" you say as you grab Chad's hand and leave the room.

As you reach the waiting room you find all of Chad and Trevor's team waiting anxiously for news. They all look up as Chad enters. He acknowledges them and tells them "We have made it in time, the doctor is saying it will be a while though, Trev is with Hannah now."

The team look relieved and settle in for the wait.

As you and Chad take a seat, Chad puts his arm around you and asks, "Hey sweetheart, how are you doing?"

"I am ok, bit tired and worried for Hannah" you respond.

"Are you hungry, do you want me to get you something from the cafeteria?"

"No, I am fine, I just want to cuddle into you darling".

"Of course, sweetie, just close your eyes, I will wake you if we hear any news" encourages Chad, as he tightens his grip on you pulling you in close,

"Thanks, I think I will try to nap a little".

You cuddle in closer resting your head on Chad's chest, closing your eyes and soon feel yourself falling asleep.

What feels like minutes later, Chad gently wakes you,

"Hey sweetheart, wake up it's time,"

You emerge from your sleep and drowsily look at Chad,

"Huh, what's going on?"

"Sweetheart, Hannah has had the baby" Chad whispers softly.

Those words wake you instantly, "What, Hannah has had the baby? how long have I been asleep?"

"It has been a couple of hours, Hannah and Trevor now have a little baby boy" replies Chad.

"Oh wow, that is great, I am so excited for them, is she and the baby Ok?"

"Yes, sweetheart, the labour went pretty quickly once Trev arrived, and Hannah and their baby boy are doing great".

"Oh fantastic" tears roll down your cheeks. "Can we see them?"

"Soon, it has just happened, they still need a little bit of time together" says Chad.

"Of course, just as long as they are safe and healthy" you say leaning into Chad.

The rest of the team are smiling and now that they have seen and congratulated Trevor they are beginning to disperse. You, Chad and Chief Wally decide to stay a little longer, until you can see the new family.

The three of you sit there chatting when a tired but ecstatic Trevor appears in the waiting room, you jump to your feet and pull him in for a hug.

"Trevor, congratulations, How are Hannah and the baby?" you ask excitedly.

"Thanks Angela, Hannah is tired but doing fantastically, and the baby is gorgeous, he has Hannah's eyes and dark hair, Hannah is asking to see you, we can't wait to show you our new son" says Trevor.

"Fantastic, we will go and see her now".

You, Chad and Wally follow Trevor to Hannah's room. As you enter the room, you see Hannah holding a gorgeous bundle. You rush towards Hannah, "Oh Hannah, congratulations" as you look down at the baby," Hannah he is beautiful".

"Thank you, Angela, he is gorgeous, isn't he?" says Hannah smiling from ear to ear. "Do you want to hold him?"

"Of course, I would love to" you say and stretch out your arms to hold the new addition.

"Oh, my goodness, he is perfect, do you have a name yet?" you ask.

Hannah responds, "Yes, we have chosen a name, we are going to call him Nathan Robert Donaldson or Nate for short".

"Oh, that is perfect, I love it".

Chad moves closer, "Guys he is gorgeous, congratulations, love the name".

"Thanks, we are so happy" replies Trevor.

Wally shakes Trevor's hand and pulls him in for a man hug, "Congratulations Trev and Hannah, he is beautiful, so relieved that everything went smoothly. I just wanted to see the baby and congratulate you both, I will let you all enjoy this time and head off".

"Thanks Wally, it means a lot" says Trevor and follows Wally to the door.

You both stay enjoying little Nate for about half an hour.

You and Chad stand up, "Well guys, we will leave you three alone now."

"Thanks Angela and Chad, so happy you were here".

As you make your way to your cars, you grab Chad's hand and look into his eyes, "Hey darling, the next time we are here, we will be meeting our own sweet babies".

"Yes, so true, it's amazing to think about, isn't it?"

CHAPTER 22

*T*he next two weeks pass, and the time has come for your first birthing class. You and Chad arrive and meet five other couples. The leader enters the room and welcomes you all. "Good evening lovely couples, my name is Olivia, and I will be guiding you over the next four weeks through the wonderful journey of childbirth."

You hear Chad giggle quietly next to you, you turn to him unable to hide your own smile, thinking not sure how wonderful the journal will be.

Olivia continues "Now we will begin by going around the room having the chance to introduce ourselves to the group and telling us what you hope to gain from attending these sessions."

All the other couples introduce themselves and it comes to you and Chad, you start "Hi everyone, my name is Angela, we are expecting twins in just over four months. I am hoping that this course will help me learn how to prepare for the birth and be the best mum I can be"

Chad squeezes your hand, and the other couples gasp at the news you are having twins, Chad introduces himself, "Hi my name is Chad, and I am wanting to learn the best way to support my wife Angela through the remainder of the pregnancy and the labour".

"Wow" says Olivia, "Twins, congratulations, how exciting for you both. Congratulations everyone on your pregnancies, now let's get started on the course content".

The remainder of the 1st hour session is spent discussing the pregnancy so far with all couples sharing their individual experiences. At the end of the session, Olivia hands everyone an information guide folder and diary and sets homework for each couple to document their pregnancy journey for the next week, in particular how they feel any issues, cravings etc.

As you farewell the other couples and head to the car to return home, Chad puts his arm around you, "Well that was really interesting, can't believe we have homework though".

"I know, I hate homework" and you both laugh, you continue "The other couples seem really friendly, it will be good to get to know them all a bit better,

"Agreed" responds Chad.

The weekend arrives and you and Chad prepare to welcome Hannah,

Trevor and baby Nate for a catch-up lunch. It has been two weeks now since Nate was born, and you have given Hannah and Trevor time to settle into parenthood. As you prepare for lunch, your excitement grows, you can't wait to hold Nate and also get some tips from Hannah on living with a newborn.

Chad enters the kitchen and prepares to help you with the meal. "How are you going sweetheart? What can I do to help out?" he asks looking around ready to help.

"Hey sweetheart, I am good, you could peel the potatoes if you like" you say giving him a kiss.

"My pleasure" says Chad, as he pulls you in close for a deep hug and kiss.

An hour later, the doorbell rings and you rush to the door to welcome the new family.

"Hey guys, come in" you say excitedly gesturing for Hannah and Trevor inside.

Once inside, you can't contain your excitement, "Let me look at Nate" you say as you excitedly look in the baby capsule and see Nate peacefully sleeping. "Oh, he is so gorgeous,"

Chad appears next to you smiling, "Oh look at him, he is beautiful guys".

Hannah and Trevor look at you smiling, "Yes, we think he is pretty darn gorgeous" say Hannah, just then Nate stirs and begins to wake up.

"Oh, he is waking up, can I hold him?" you ask.

"Of course, Nate can't wait to see his Aunty Angela" says Hannah.

You reach into the capsule and gently lift Nate out and place him in your arms cuddling him close. Nate looks up at you with his big green eyes. As you hold him, you notice Chad watching you, smiling. After a few minutes, Chad whispers to you, "Can I hold him now?"

"Of course," you respond as you gently pass Nate over to Chad and watch him smiling and gently rocking Nate in his arms, all the while excitedly thinking how wonderful it will be watching Chad with your own babies.

The oven timer begins to sound, snapping you out of your daydreams.

"Oh, lunch is ready" and you make your way to the kitchen, Hannah follows you leaving the men together.

"So, Hannah, how are you going" you ask concerned.

"Angela, it is surreal, he is such a good baby really, sure he has his times when he screams the place down, but overall, he is such a happy little boy.

"Oh, that is great Hannah," you say smiling.

"I have to be honest though, it is not all roses, it is so different and takes a while to get used to, I am so tired, Thank goodness I have Trev, he is amazing, and helps with the bottle feeding and changing so I can get some sleep. I don't know what I will do without him when he goes back to work after his paternity leave".

"Oh, I understand" you say trying to reassure her, "It is only natural that you feel a bit lost and overwhelmed, it will take time to settle down".

You both finish serving up lunch and return to the dining room with the plates. Trevor places Nate back in his capsule covering him up, kisses him on the forehead and joins you all at the table for lunch.

While enjoying lunch, Trevor and Hannah can't stop beaming as they relive stories of the last two weeks with baby Nate. As you all finish the main meal, Hannah looks at Trevor with a nervous grin and then turns to you and Chad.

"Angela and Chad, we have something we need to talk to you about".

You and Chad both look intently at Hannah, and you say, "Of course, what is it?"

Hannah continues, "Ok, well do you remember my cousin Marcus, who lives in Melbourne?" You think for a bit, and then nod, "Of course I remember him".

"Well, Marcus is getting married in a couple of weeks and he has invited Trevor and I".

"Oh, that is great" you say.

"Yes, well we want to go" Hannah continues and takes a deep breath, "We were hoping that you both could look after Nate for the weekend while we are away?"

You look at Chad, and his face lights up, you both turn to Hannah and Trevor and say at the same time "Of course"

"Really, are you sure?" says Trevor.

"Of course, mate, we would love to look after the little guy," says Chad,

Hannah looks relieved, "Thanks guys, that is so great of you both, I would have asked Mum, but obviously she is coming to the wedding too, and

Trev's parents live a long distance away".

You respond, "That is exciting, can't wait to have him stay with us".

Trevor looks at you both and laughs, "Hey guys, it will be like a practice session for when your babies come".

"Yes, of course" Chad responds smiling.

After you all finish lunch, you and Hannah clear the table and clean the dishes while the boys work on setting up some of the furniture for the nursery that recently arrived.

As Chad and Trevor start working in the nursery, Chad takes this time to ask Trevor some questions that have been on his mind for a while.

"So, Trevor, what is like being a Dad?" Chad asks.

"Oh buddy, it is fantastic, it is the best thing to happen to me, apart from meeting Hannah of course. Hannah is a wonderful mum".

"Oh great, I am so happy for you, buddy I have to ask you a personal question, did you find Hannah's sex drive change during pregnancy?" Chad asks.

"Oh yeah, for sure, especially early on, she was much more into sex than ever before, why have you noticed a change in Angela?"

"Well yes actually, once the morning sickness eased, her libido definitely increased, and our sex life really ramped back up" says Chad smiling.

"Ok, well that is good then" laughs Trevor.

Trevor thinks for a little while, and then says "Buddy, one piece of advice I will give you, as Angela moves into the 3rd trimester, brush up on your massage skills, she will welcome back and feet massages, I became very adept at massage by the time Nate was born,"

"Oh yes, I have already been told to perform regular massages already" laughs Chad.

After the kitchen is cleaned you and Hannah move to the lounge and chat. As you hold baby Nate, you turn to Hannah and ask, "So Hannah, what is it really like being a mum now?"

Hannah looks at you and answers, "It is weird really, to have this beautiful little boy so totally reliant on you is an unreal feeling. I am feeling better physically now, I was quite sore early on, but that has gone now. Angela, I tell you, it was scary at first, but I wouldn't change a thing, it is the best thing I have ever done, and I can't believe how much I love this little boy."

You nod to Hannah smiling.

Hannah continues, "Don't worry Angela, you will be a natural at motherhood".

You both spend time catching up on your work and life in general. As Nate is peacefully sleeping, you decide the time is right to prepare afternoon tea, you make your way down to the nursery to let the boys now that snacks are served. As you approach the nursery room door, you hear Chad and Trevor talking.

"Hey Trev, Can I ask you one other thing, How was Hannah when she was pregnant? I mean how were her mood swings?" Chad asks.

"Oh yeah, the mood swings were something else, I remember once that Hannah didn't talk to me for a whole day because I forgot to replace the toilet paper roll" Trevor respond laughing.

"Oh, I can see how that could be annoying" Chad laughs, "Seriously though, the mood swings are hard to negotiate, I mean Angela is getting a bit better as the pregnancy is progressing, but it is hard to know the right thing to say or do sometimes, she cried once because I finished the last chocolate bar, Oh and the food cravings are unbelievable, the other day, Angela was eating bananas and tomato sauce" Chad laughs

"Oh, that is odd, don't think I could come at that" Trevor responds with a screwed-up face, "Hannah had some weird cravings as well, one day I found her eating pickles and ice-cream".

"Interesting" Chad responds laughing.

"Chad, it will get easier, just try to understand that she doesn't mean it, she is going through stuff that us blokes will never understand, we just have to be there as best we can and support them".

"Thanks Trev, that makes sense".

You wait another couple of minutes and then enter the nursery, "Hey guys, how is everything going in here, are you ready to take a break and have some afternoon tea, Oh wow, you have done a great job setting up the cribs and change table, looks fabulous."

"Oh, hi sweetheart, so glad we have gotten these put together, but definitely ready for a break" Chad says smiling and pulling you in for a hug.

As you follow Trevor and Chad back to the lounge, you can't help thinking about what you heard Chad say and feel guilty. You try to think of how to make it up to Chad.

Shortly after afternoon tea, Nate wakes up and becomes unsettled, Hannah and Trevor have to leave and take Nate home. After you bid farewell you and Chad return to the lounge, you sit down next to Chad and grab his hand. "Hey sweetheart, I have been thinking, you have been so good to me through this pregnancy, I know at times I have been difficult at times, why don't we go away for a romantic weekend together before the babies come?"

Chad squeezes your hand and smiles, "What are you talking about sweetheart? you have been fine. A weekend away does sounds great though".

"I heard you and Trev talking earlier, I am sorry for being moody, I didn't mean to be difficult,"

Chad puts his fingers to your lips "Stop, you have not been difficult, I understand that you are going through a lot with this pregnancy, looking after me when I was recovering and all your work stuff.. Sometimes it has been a little hard, but I understand sweetheart, you are amazing."

"Thanks sweetheart, I love you".

"I love you too of course, so did you have anywhere in mind for our weekend away?" Chad asks.

"You decide, it is up to you, wherever you want to go, I just want to be with you" you say resting your head on Chad's chest.

"Ok I will have a think about it" Chad says as he pulls you in close.

CHAPTER 23

*T*he weekend that you will be looking after Nate has arrived and you are preparing the house for Hannah and Trevor to arrive.

The doorbell rings and you and Chad rush excitedly to the door.

"Hello, come in" you say to Hannah and Trevor

They follow you into the lounge room and begin to unload their stash of supplies. You and Chad look at each other in surprise, there are nappies, bags of clothes, formula bottles.

Chad asks "Wow, that is a lot of stuff".

Trevor replies, "This is not all of it, can you help me with the rest of the stuff in the car".

"Oh, yeah of course" Chad says, he follows Trevor out to the car and raises his eyebrows to you.

Smiling you turn to Hannah, "We are so excited to have little Nate for the weekend".

"Thanks Angela, we are so grateful for this" replies Hannah as she adjusts Nates blanket in his carrier. "Now, I will warn you, he has been a little fussy the last couple of days, but we have had him at the medical centre, and he checks out fine".

"Oh ok" you respond, a little concerned.

Trevor and Chad return inside with a crib, and portable baby rocker".

Hannah turns to you, "I decided to bring Nate's own crib, as he is used to it and thought it might help him settle".

"Oh yes of course, that makes sense, let's set him up in our room, so we can keep him close to us".

Chad and Trevor make their way to your room and proceed to set up the crib.

Hannah hands you a notebook, "I have written down some notes on his routine to keep him settled. Here are some bottles of formula, plus some extra with instructions on how to mix it up".

"Thanks Hannah, we will be fine".

"I know, I am just so nervous, this is the first time I have left Nate".

"I know, Chad and I are so excited to look after him, we have been looking forward to it since you first asked" you pull Hannah in for a hug.

Just then, Trevor and Chad return, "Everything is all set up for the little guy" says Chad smiling.

Trevor turns to Hannah, "We better get going soon, we have a long day ahead".

"Yes true, I know, we have to leave" says Hannah.

Nate stirs slightly, Hannah reaches down and plants a big kiss on his little head. "You be a good boy, for Aunty Angela and Uncle Chad, Mum and Dad will miss you, we will be back in two days, sweet boy, love you".

You see tears forming in her eyes, you reach out and squeeze her hand and smile reassuringly.

Trevor also leans down to baby Nate, gives him a kiss on his forehead, "Bye little buddy, be a good boy".

Nate gurgles in response.

Trevor puts his arm around Hannah and heads towards the door, before leaving Hannah says, "Call us if you need anything at all, thank you again".

"We will, now you two get going and have a safe trip, we will be fine" you say, giving Hannah and Trevor a hug goodbye.

Chad follows you to the door and waves goodbye, "Have a great time you guys".

As you close the door, you turn to Chad and smile, "Well, it is real now, he is here".

Chad nods and you both return to Nate. He looks up at you and he gurgles in response.

"Hey sweetheart, you are going to be with us for the next couple of days, are you excited" you ask as you pick up Nate and cuddle him close.

Chad notices the notebook on the kitchen counter,

"What is this?" he asks as he picks it up and starts to flick through it.

"Oh, that is the instruction manual" you respond laughing.

"Oh good, we will need that" says Chad smiling.

"No, we will be fine, won't we gorgeous boy" you say as you look down at Nate.

Chad joins you and you both sit on the couch watching Nate,

A little while later Nate begins to get restless and starts to cry. You head over to him and pick him up.

"What is wrong little man?" you check the schedule that Hannah left, he is not quite due for a bottle yet. As you cuddle him, you notice that his nappy feels a bit full,

"Oh buddy, you need a fresh nappy, come on let's go, Chad can you bring me some nappies please".

"Of course," Chad picks up a pack of nappies and follows you to the bedroom. As you undress Nate, you both are confronted with the extent of the little boy's nappy.

"Oh wow, that is intense" says Chad, as he hands you the nappies and turns to leave.

"Hey, where are you going?" you question Chad,

Chad responds sheepishly, "Oh, I thought you had this under control".

You laugh, "No you can help with this, we need practice".

Chad comes closer, "Of course, let me help".

Just as you begin to clean little Nate and get his new nappy ready, Nate begins to urinate all over your arm, and down the front of your top.

"Oh heck," you cry out as you reach for a cloth and cover Nate and grab another cloth and begin to wipe yourself.

 "Hey buddy good shot" Chad says to Nate, breaking into laughter.

Nate smiles back very happy with himself.

You can't help but laugh as well, as you continue to wipe yourself down.

You both then successfully change Nate's nappy; Nate is happy now and you change your clothes and then both return to the lounge. You put Nate back in his capsule and he is content and quickly returns to sleep.

The sound of a message comes through on your phone, as you check it, is a message from Hannah.

"Hey Angela, how are you going? How is Nate?"

You respond, "He is doing great; he has a fresh nappy and his is having a little nap now".

"Good, he is due for a bottle in about an hour" Hannah responds.

"All good, we will be set".

As if on clockwork, an hour later, Nate wakes up from his nap, and cries, each cry becomes more intense.

Chad looks worried, "Is he ok?" he asks as he reaches to pick him up trying to console him.

"He is hungry, he is due for a bottle now, can you hold him while I organise the bottle?"

"Of course," responds Chad as he gently rocks Nate trying to settle him, but to no avail.

You follow the instructions detailed by Hannah and return to Chad with the bottle.

"Oh, can I try him with the bottle?" Chad asks,

"Of course," you hand him the bottle and watch him feed baby Nate smiling. You and Chad can't help smiling as you both watch Nate eagerly take the bottle.

"Oh, he is loving the bottle isn't he" says Chad excitedly.

"Yes, he must have been very hungry".

Chad continues to feed Nate, once he finishes, Chad begins to rock him,

"Careful sweetheart don't rock him too much, he has just eaten" you say.

Chad replies, "Don't worry he will be ....," before he can finish his sentence, Nate vomits all over himself and down Chad's chest. "Oh no crap, sorry buddy," Chad says as he stops rocking Nate.

"See I tried to warn you" you reply laughing. "Now we are even, aren't we?", you hand Chad some cloths to help clean himself and Nate.

"Yes, very true" Chad laughs as he dabs his shirt.

You clean up Nate, while Chad changes.

The rest of the night is spent cuddling and watching Nate and then it is time to retire for the night, you give Nate another fresh nappy and lay him to rest for the evening, in the crib next to your bed, he quickly drifts off to sleep and both you and Chad decide to head to bed.

As you lay in bed, Chad cuddles up behind you, caresses your baby bump and whispers in your ear, "It will only be a few more short months and then it will be our babies we will be settling down for the night".

"Yes, I am so excited about it", You snuggle into Chad and you both join Nate and drift off to sleep.

After a couple of hours, you and Chad are jolted awake by Nate's cries, half asleep you head over to his crib and pick him up. Chad wakes up also, "Is he Ok?" he asks concerned.

"Yes, I think so, I will check his nappy and hopefully he will settle again".

After changing his nappy, you try to settle Nate again, but he is still crying loudly.

"Wow, he is a loud little man, isn't he?" Chad laughs as he joins you at Nates crib.

"Yeah, maybe he needs another bottle?"

"Let me organise it" Chad says as he sleepily heads to the kitchen, Just as he reaches the doorway, he stubs his toe on the doorframe and cries out rubbing his foot, "Ouch, I hit my toe on the doorway,

Nate is still crying loudly, "Oh are you Ok sweetheart? you ask looking at Chad.

"Yeah, just really hurts" Chad responds as he hobbles to the kitchen to prepare Nate's bottle. While you wait for him to return, you pick up Nate and unsuccessfully try to rock him to console him.

After what seems like an eternity, Chad finally returns with Nate's bottle and Nate eagerly latches on.

"Oh, thank goodness, he has stopped crying now" you say as you watch Nate drink his bottle.

Once Nate finishes his bottle, you burp him and then place back into his crib and he quietly drifts off to sleep again,

You and Chad quietly return to bed and fall back asleep only to be woken up a few hours later by Nate crying again. You sleepily stretch and climb out of bed, noticing the bedside clock reading 4am and make your way to Nate's crib, pick him up and gently rock him to soothe him. Chad joins you, "Is he Ok?" he asks.

"I think he just needs to have a fresh nappy" you reply as you make your way to the change table.

A few minutes later, Nate is all changed and ready to settle back down to sleep. You and Chad climb back into bed and quickly fall back to sleep.

The sound of your phone is the next to wake you up, you quickly answer it before it has a chance to wake Nate.

"Hello Angela, it's Hannah, How is my boy going?"

"Hi Hannah," you try to fight back a yawn, "He is doing really well, he is still sleeping right now".

Just as you say that Nate begins to stir in his crib, you nudge Chad awake and point him towards Nate. Chad yawns and climbs out of bed and makes his way to pick up Nate and bring him back to bed.

Hannah continues, "Oh I am so glad he is ok; we miss him so much. How did he sleep for you overnight"?

"He woke up a couple of times, but we managed to settle him fairly quickly."

"Oh, that is good, I am so relieved" says Hannah.

"So, Hannah how was the flight yesterday?"

"We had a good trip, arrived late yesterday afternoon, we have to start getting ready for the wedding soon, the ceremony starts at about 11am, What have you got planned for the day?"

"We might go for a walk later".

"Oh good, have a great time, I better go and start getting ready, remember to call if you need anything".

"No worries, we will be fine, enjoy the wedding, see you tomorrow".

You hang up and turn to Chad, he is cuddling Nate.

"Good morning sweetheart, that was Hannah, just checking on Nate" you say smiling.

"Good morning," replies Chad, looking sleepy as he rocks Nate gently. After making a bottle for Nate, you both lay back in bed with Nate in between you, watching him as he falls back to sleep.

Later that day, as Nate wakes up, you and Chad decide to take a short walk in the sun of a mild winter's day.

The remainder of the day goes by easily, Nate is settled, and you both enjoy spending time with him all the while dreaming of when your own babies arrive.

As you get ready to retire for the night, Nate enjoys his bottle and easily drifts off to sleep. You and

Chad both head off to bed wondering how long before Nate wakes again. As if on a repeat from the previous night, Nate wakes up again crying only after a short two-hour sleep. Chad turns on the bedside lamp and turns to you, "Sweetheart, you stay there, I will go to him".

You smile at him, pull up the covers "Thank you sweetheart, let me know if you need help".

Chad makes his way over to Nate, as he reaches into the crib, he picks him up "Hey little buddy, what's going on? Oh, I see, you need a new nappy don't you".

Chad makes his way to the change table, cleans up Nate and then rocks him until he settles and drifts back off to sleep. He gently puts Nate back in his crib, covers him warmly, as Chad climbs back into bed, you embrace him, kiss him smiling, "You are a natural sweetheart, you got him back to sleep easily".

Chad kisses you on the forehead, "Thank you Darling".

You both settle down and drift back to sleep for a few more hours until Nate wakes again for his next bottle.

Before you know it the time for Hannah and Trevor to return arrives, Hannah rushes through the door straight to Nate, picking him up in her arms, "Oh baby, I missed you so much, Mummy's home now, so Angela, how was he?"

"Hannah, he was wonderful, we loved looking after him".

"Oh, thank you so much".

You all spend the next hour or so catching up, chatting about the wedding and your time with Nate.

Hannah looks at Trevor, "Well honey, we better get this little guy home and let Angela and Chad have some peace".

"Yeah of course, I will start getting his things in the car" replies Trevor.

"I will help you buddy" replies Chad.

After the car has been packed, you bid farewell to Hannah, Trevor and baby Nate. After cleaning up, you join Chad on the couch. "Wow it is so quiet now that Nate has gone home, I miss him" you say as you rest your head on Chad's chest.

Chad pulls you into his arms tightly, "Yeah, I know what you mean, he is a great little guy".

CHAPTER 24

*T*he time for your weekend away finally arrives, you have both decided to head north up the coast. Chad is an avid surfer, so is looking forward to catching some waves. Chad gently wakes you from your sleep, "Sweetie, time to get up, we need to get going early to miss the morning traffic".

Reluctantly, you open your eyes open, stretching "Good morning honey" you say smiling.

A little while later, with your car packed, both you and Chad are all set to head off on your last trip together before your babies arrive. You turn to Chad asking, "Ready to go?"

"Absolutely, been looking forward to this since you mentioned it" Chad answers smiling, he leans over and kisses you,

After driving for a little over an hour, Chad unexpectedly pulls the car over. You turn to Chad and ask, "Why have we stopped, everything ok?"

"Yes, everything is fine, the sun will be rising shortly, I thought we could sit and watch it together" Chad replies.

"Oh, that sounds like a great idea", you both hop out of the car, Chad places a travel blanket on the grass area of the lookout, helps you to sit down and holds you in his arm and together you settle in to watch the sun rise.

A few minutes later, the horizon explodes with an amazing combination of pink and gold as the sun begins to peep over the horizon, As you snuggle deeper into Chad's arms, you whisper to him, "This is gorgeous, I have never seen such a beautiful sunrise before"

Chad deepens his embrace, kisses the top of your head, and replies, "It is amazing, so wonderful to share this with you."

You both remain watching the sun rise for another half an hour, chatting about the plans for your weekend, and your babies. Finally, Chad says, "Well love, we better get back on the road, still got a long way to go until we reach our destination".

"Yes, I guess we better get back on the road" you respond with a sigh. As Chad helps you up, you feel your babies move, you jump a little, place your hands on your now large baby bump, smiling you say "Oh, the babies are awake now!" you grab Chad's hand, place it on your stomach.

Chad smiles, "Good morning darlings, Oh, you sure are both active this morning aren't you".

"Yes, they must be excited about our weekend away, no matter how often I feel them, it is always so special and makes me so happy" you say to Chad.

"I know what you mean, it is an amazing feeling" Chad responds, keeping one hand on your stomach, he pulls you towards him in a deep embrace and kisses you deeply".

You both make your way back to the car and continue the drive. The sun is shining brightly now, and the sky is a beautiful blue with wispy clouds adding to the beauty.

Several hours later, Chad finally pulls up in front of the lovely quaint beachside cottage that will be your home for the next two days.

"Oh wow, this is beautiful, just what it looked like on the brochure and website" you say as you get out of the car.

"It is lovely, and it is right on the beach, look at those waves, I can't wait to get out there" Chad responds smiling.

Chad brings the suitcases inside. As you follow him inside, your breath is taken away, "Oh this is gorgeous" you say as your look around. It is beautifully decorated with comfortable old-fashioned furniture.

As you make your way to the bedroom, you see a lovely four poster bed, with luxurious plush bed furnishing. You rush forward and make yourself comfortable on the bed. "Oh wow, this bed is amazing, so soft and luxurious, not sure I will ever want to leave this bed" you say to Chad with a wink.

Chad joins you on the bed, smiling "Oh really?".

You pull Chad in for a deep kiss, he lays you down on the bed, lays down next to you and deepens the kiss, you both begin to caress each other. Chad moves his hands from your neck, down your chest gently squeezing your breasts, his hands then move down to your baby bump and then he places his hand under your shirt to caress your skin, continually kissing you passionately and deeply.

With your hand, you move over Chad's chest and arms feeling the taut muscles under his shirt, before long your hands move down to the top of his pants finding the zipper, you pull the zip down and reach inside to find his length becoming firmer with every stroke. Before long, you are both naked and skin to skin, both becoming more aroused with each stroke of each other's bodies. Chad breaks from the kiss and whispers to you, "Sweetheart, get on your knees, I want to enter you from behind".

You respond my turning over and supporting yourself on your knees, Chad begins to caress you between your legs, massaging your folds with firm pressure that excites you with every stroke. You soon feel his firm length at your entrance, you gasp with pleasure as he enters you and you feel his rhythmic motion fill you. He supports your baby belly with his strong hand, the other hand caresses your breasts sending delight all through your body. You grab the bed linen in your hands as you ride the wave of pleasure, audible moans can be heard from both of you as you both reach the climax.

As you both come down from your high, you lay in each other's arms.

Finally, you break the silence, "That was fantastic, I love you so much".

"I love you too sweetheart" responds Chad as he kisses the top of your head "Are you hungry darling, do you want to go and get some dinner?"

"Yeah, I am getting hungry, we better get up and head into town for dinner". So, you both get dressed and head into town to enjoy a romantic meal together at a local restaurant.

The next morning you both wake up to the sound of the waves crashing on the shore across the road from your holiday unit. The sun is shining through the window spreading golden light throughout the room. As you open your eyes, you turn and reach for Chad only to find his side of the bed empty. Sitting up you look around the room searching for him. As you get out of bed you hear noises coming from the kitchen area, Chad is in the kitchen and is cooking up a special breakfast of bacon and eggs for you both. As you enter the kitchen, Chad looks up and smiles "Good morning sweetheart, sorry if I woke you".

"Good morning, Darling, no you didn't wake me, do you need any help?

"No, all good, just sit there and I will serve you,"

"Thank you, that is so lovely, what are you wanting to do today?"

"Well, after breakfast, I would love to go surfing and try and catch some waves".

"Oh, that sounds great, I will join you at the beach and watch you".

You both enjoy the delicious breakfast, clean up the kitchen and then get ready to head over to the beach. The sun is shining warmly, and you find a patch of sand, Chad lays down a blanket for you, helps you down, and then grabs his board, kisses you and heads off into the water.

You watch him paddle out and prepare to surf the waves as they come crashing into shore. Before you realise it a couple of hours has passed, and Chad rejoins you on the sand.

"You looked great out there" you say to Chad as he grabs a towel and starts to pat himself dry.

"Oh, it was fantastic, it has been so long since I have been able to surf like that, I could have spent all day out there".

After spending more time sitting on the sand enjoying the fresh sea air,

Chad turns to you and asks, "What do you want to do for the rest of the day Darling?".

"We could go into town and check out the craft shops etc".

"Absolutely, let's go and get cleaned up and check out the town" says Chad as he stretches out his arms and helps you up from the sand.

Walking down the main street, you excitedly look at all the small shops. Inside a small arcade you both come across an antique store, inside is some restored furniture. You and Chad enter and start to look around when suddenly you see a draw set in the corner, you grab Chad's hand and head over to see it more closely. It is white in colour with stencilled blue and pink flowers and beautiful glass handles. "Oh Chad, look at this, this is beautiful" you say as you rub your hands over the top of the draw set.

"Wow, it is lovely, isn't it?"

"It would look great in the nursery, don't you think?" you ask Chad excitedly.

"Yeah, I guess so" replies Chad, just as a salesperson comes over to meet you.

"Hello, welcome, how are you today? My name is Toby, How can I assist you today".

Chad responds, "Hi Toby, we are interested in this draw set".

"Ah yes, this just come in a little while ago, it has been tastefully restored" says Toby.

"Yes, we are interested in this set for our baby nursery" you say.

"Congratulations, yes this would be wonderful for you, Wait a minute, I think we also have a matching change table, let me have a look for you" says Toby as he quickly heads over to the other side of the shop.

You look at Chad with a smile,

Shortly after Toby returns, "Yes we have a matching change table, we could do a deal, both of them for $250.00?"

Chad looks at you and sees your excited face, "You have a deal Toby, we will take them both".

You hug Chad in excitement.

The next morning, you and Chad prepare to head home after your short break away. As you pack the last of your belongings into the car, you pull Chad in for a kiss, "Thank you for a great weekend away, it was great".

"Yes, it was a great break" replies Chad.

CHAPTER 25

It has been a couple of weeks since you and Chad had your break away, and you close to reaching your 7 month of pregnancy. The final stages of pregnancy are taking their toll, you are very uncomfortable and beginning to feel quite breathless and tired and can't wait for the arrival of your two little ones.

As you are sitting in your office working on the marketing proposal for the new client, you hear a knock on the door and look up to see Greta standing in the doorway.

"Hi Greta, How are you?" you ask smiling.

"Hi Angela, I am ok, but we need to talk about the account for the Anderson Group" Greta replies and makes her way inside your office and takes a seat.

"Ok, sure what is going on?" you ask.

"Well unfortunately, the client is unhappy with the proposal we put forward and needs it revised immediately".

"Oh Ok, what is the problem?" you ask concerned.

Greta continues, "They are not happy with the costings of the print and TV advertising, and want us to reduce the costings by at least 20%"

"I will have a look at it, but we tried to be minimal with the print media, we could try to reduce some of the publications, and perhaps reduce the TV commercial schedule" you reply as you bring up their file on your computer.

"Ok, Angela, can you please rework the costing for this proposal and get something together by the end of today. This account is very important as they will be repeat customers and have a large customer base, that we are hoping to tap into."

"Of course, I understand Greta, leave it with me" you reply.

"Thanks Angela, we will need to have the amended proposal by the end of the day so Rick and present it at the meeting tomorrow.

"No problem, I will get onto it now".

Thank you Angela" Greta responds as she gets up and heads out the door.

As you sit at your desk, you think to yourself, "Well, that is just great, how I am going to fix this now".

You spend the remainder of the day, glued to your computer screen, tossing around figures, rearranging strategies and finally come up with an amended proposal. You feel exhausted as you put the final touches to the proposal and email it through to Greta and Rick for review.

As you pack up your office and get ready to leave to head home, you pass Greta in the corridor.

"Hi Greta, I have just emailed the amended Anderson Group proposal to you and Rick".

"Excellent, thank you Angela, Rick and I will have a look at it now. Are you heading home?"

"Yes, It has been a long day, feel like I am getting a bit of migraine now, see you tomorrow".

"For sure, take care, you do look a bit pale, go home have a rest, thanks for your efforts".

You head home, Chad is on shift tonight, so you make a quick snack for dinner, catch up on some of your favourite TV shows and still having a headache decide to head to bed early hoping to feel better the next day.

As you awake the next morning, you still feel the headache from the day before, you push through and head into the office, anxious to discover how Rick felt about the amended proposal you prepared yesterday.

After arriving at the office, you head towards your office. After setting down your bags, you search for Greta, to discover whether your hard work from yesterday was received by Rick. You find Greta in the staff kitchen.

"Good morning, Greta, how are you?"

"Hi Angela, I am good how are you going?" replies Greta smiling.

You find relief in Greta's smile, hoping it means that your proposal was good, "I am doing Ok, just a bit tired and still have that headache from yesterday, Did Rick look at the new proposal I sent late yesterday?" you ask.

"Yes, Rick and I checked your proposal and were very impressed in what you put together in such a short time frame yesterday. Rick will be presenting this to Anderson Group early this afternoon."

"Oh, that is good to hear" you reply relieved. You fill your water bottle and return to your office to begin your day. You are still struggling with a headache, you would prefer not to take a Panadol especially while pregnant, so you try to push through.

A couple of hours later, you hear a knock on your door and Derrick appears. "Good morning, Angela, how are you going?"

"Oh, Hi Derrick, I am good, just a bit tired, and have a whopping headache, How are you?"

"I am doing really well, I need to update the programs on your computer, is it ok if I do that now?"

"Oh yes, sure, go for it".

"Great, it should not take too long" says Derrick as he makes his way to your computer.

"No worries, How are you and Bree going?" you ask.

"Bree and I are doing really well, actually, I am bursting to tell you, Bree has just found out that she is pregnant, we were going to wait to tell anyone, but I am so excited".

"Oh Derrick, that is fantastic news, I am so happy for you".

"Thanks Angela, Can you pass me the notebook I left on the shelf over there?"

"Sure, no worries" as you stand up, the headache that you have been feeling all morning gets stronger and you suddenly feel very weak, you stand still for a moment trying to steady yourself. You vaguely hear Derrick ask, "Angela are you ok?"

"No not really" you shakily respond and then everything goes black.

The next thing you remember, is waking up in a hospital bed, with Chad holding your hand looking worried.

"Oh sweetheart, hey, you are awake" says Chad as he caresses your hand.

"What happened?" you ask.

"You collapsed at work, Derrick and Greta rushed you here to the hospital, the doctor has run some tests, just waiting for her to come back with the results, you had me so worried sweetheart" says Chad as he reaches to kiss you.

"Are the babies, ok?" you ask worriedly.

"Yes, Yes they are fine, but the doc is worried why you collapsed, she did mention that your blood pressure was pretty high, so that was a concern, how are you feeling now?"

"I am pretty tired, and still have an intense headache".

"Just rest sweetheart, I will sit here with you" says Chad as he caresses your hair.

You close your eyes and drift off to sleep for a little while until the doctor comes in.

"Hi Angela, how are you feeling?" asks the doctor as she looks through your file.

"Hi doctor, I am still feeling quite weak, and the headache is still pretty bad".

"Yes, well we have your results here" responds the doctor.

Chad takes your hand and you both look at the doctor awaiting her news.

Well Angela, we are quite concerned about your blood pressure, it is quite high at the moment. The test results indicate that you may have the condition called Preeclampsia".

"Oh, that is not good, is it?" you ask.

"Angela, it is quite serious, how have your stress levels been of late?" asks the doctor.

"Well, it has been a huge few months, what with Chad's accident, recovery, my friend Hannah's baby shower that I had to organise and also, I have been under a bit of pressure at work, trying to sort out our larger accounts prior to me taking maternity leave." you reply.

"Yes, you certainly have had your fair share of difficulties during this pregnancy for sure, The stress certainly would have been a contributing factor, Luckily we appear to have diagnosed this quickly, so the outlook is good, Angela, it is not all good news though" says the doctor. "This condition is quite serious, as you are nearing the end of your pregnancy and as you are carrying twins, you will need to remain on complete rest for the remainder of your pregnancy".

"Oh, really, do you mean bed rest?" you ask.

"No not complete bed rest, but you will need to stop working now and stay home and do as little as possible, although I will not confine you to complete bed rest, you must rest as much as possible".

"Oh, that won't be a problem, I will make sure she rests" says Chad. "Are the babies ok?"

"Yes, the babies are healthy, as long as Angela remains on semi bed rest for the remainder of her pregnancy, she should be ok".

"When can I take her home doctor?" asks Chad.

"Considering the circumstances, I want to keep Angela in hospital for at least the next 2 days to monitor her, if her blood pressure reduces and remains stable, we can discuss releasing her home to continue enforced rest. So as mentioned, she will not need to be on complete bed rest, but she will need to rest as much as possible."

"Oh ok, can I work from home, if I work from bed? there is a new client proposal I need to finish".

"Angela, I am sorry, you will need to stop working immediately and pass this proposal on to someone else, you are to rest as much as possible, no stress etc".

"Oh no, I will have to tell Greta and Rick, the proposal was due at the end of this week".

Two days later, Chad arrives at the hospital to take you home, the doctor comes in to give you a final check before discharging you.

"Hi Angela and Chad, we are very happy with how you have recovered from your recent scare. Your blood pressure and all other vitals are back in the safe ranges now. How do you feel overall Angela" asks the doctor.

"I am feeling much better, the headache has gone, and I don't feel nearly as weak as I was a few days ago, I am really excited about going home, Oh, no offence doctor, you all have been wonderful".

"That's great to hear Angela, and no offence taken, I understand that you are very keen to get home" laughs the doctor.

The doctor turns to Chad, "Now Chad, as I mentioned the other day, it is very important that Angela remain as calm and rested as possible for the remainder of her pregnancy".

"That will not be a problem, I have everything sorted, she will be well looked after" replies Chad.

"Great, then I don't see any reason to keep you hear any longer, I have made an appointment for you to come back and see me next week, and the appointments will be weekly for the remainder of your pregnancy, so we can keep an eye on your blood pressure and vitals, but as always, if there is any problems or concerns at all, please come back as soon as possible"

"Thanks Doctor, we will" you reply.

With that the doctor signs the discharge papers, and bids you both farewell and leaves you and Chad to gather your belongings, wait for an orderly to come with a wheelchair to escort you to the car.

As you arrive home, your phone rings, it is Hannah,

"Hi love, are you home, are you ok, I am so worried about you" asks Hannah.

"Hi, yes we just got home, I am ok, a little tired, but so glad to be home."

"Oh, that is so good, I will leave you to rest, I will come and visit you tomorrow if that is, ok? call me if you and Chad need anything at all Ok".

"Thanks Hannah, I would love to see you and Nate tomorrow, looking forward to it, I will be here" you reply laughing.

"Great, I will call you in the morning when I am on my way, now go and rest up, see you tomorrow. Bye."

"Bye Hannah"

"Was that Hannah?" Chad asks as he emerges from the kitchen with a snack for you both.

"Yes, it was, she is coming around tomorrow".

"Oh, that is great, Now as I am still having to work at the moment, I have organised a bit of a roster system with Hannah, your Mum and mine to come and be with you when I have to work" says Chad.

"Oh, that is sweet, but really not necessary, I will be fine by myself" you reply, but Chad cuts you off mid-sentence.

"No, I won't take any chances with you or the babies, I want to make sure someone is here with you at all times Ok, we won't take no for an answer on this Ok" Chad looks at you sweetly but sternly at the same time.

Reluctantly you agree, and you both settle in on the couch to watch some TV and DVD's that Chad has picked out.

CHAPTER 26

Several weeks have passed since your health scare and you are beginning to get very bored with being restricted to being at home constantly. You want to go out in the late winter sunshine and enjoy a gentle stroll around the neighbourhood or visit the shops for some retail therapy. Just as your mind wanders to the outdoors, Hannah and Nate arrive for their pre-planned monitoring session.

"Good Morning, Angela, How are we all feeling today" says Hannah as she bounds into the room.

Unable to hide your feelings you reply "Yeah, Hi, I am so bored of sitting home here".

"Yeah, I understand, but you know why right? Anyway, Nate and I are here now, so no more sad face ok"

Hannah replies with a smile to try to lift your mood.

You force a smile and sigh.

Hannah places Nate in your arms and continues "Right now that Chad has gone to work, you and I need to plan your baby shower, Are you ready?"

"Wait, what, how can I have a baby shower when I stuck here on rest?"

"No fear, lovely, I got Chad to ask the doctor if it would be ok, and after checking your latest results she said it would be OK, as long as you do nothing, but sit and enjoy yourself for the afternoon." replies Hannah as she pulls out a notebook and pen to begin jotting down plans for the shower.

"Oh, I am not really sure, I am in the mood to plan anything today" you respond.

"Nonsense, it will be good for you to have something else to focus on besides being stuck inside feeling sorry for yourself "replies Hannah insistently.

You realise that there is no use resisting Hannah, you have known her for too long and know that once she sets her mind to something, there is no changing it.

Smiling, you relinquish to Hannah, "Ok, but on one condition, the sun is shining out, can we at least go outside for a bit and enjoy the fresh air and sun?"

Hannah, looks outside and says "Ok, let me just put on Nate's parker and hat, so he doesn't get cold out".

So, you both make your way outside and sit in the sun and begin to plan the upcoming baby shower.

A couple of hours later, you have finalised the guest list, party food, games etc, enjoyed a lovely picnic lunch and your mood has improved.

"Thanks Hannah, I needed this today, I am feeling better".

"Excellent, glad I could help, now the wind is picking up a bit, we better get this little guy back inside and I will make a start on organising some dinner."

"Are you sure? you don't have to stay all day here, I will be fine, Chad will be home later tonight, you must want to get home yourself".

"Nonsense, I will only be going home to an empty house anyway, as Trev is also on shift, Nate and I might as well stay with you, besides, Chad would have my head, if I left you alone" Hannah replies with a laugh.

"Thanks Hannah, I really appreciate it", you squeeze her hand in thanks.

The rest of the day is spent watching TV, playing with Nate and catching up on well needed girl chat.

Before you know it, Chad and Trevor walk through the door.

"Good evening, ladies, how was your day?" asks Chad as he makes his way over to you on the couch for a kiss and hug.

"Hi guys, we have had a great day, Hannah has been amazing".

"Oh, that is great to hear, thanks Hannah" Chad replies smiling.

Hannah and Trevor stay for a little while longer and then head home for the evening.

"You certainly look a lot happier tonight?" says Chad.

"Yes, having Hannah here was just what I needed today" you reply as you settle into bed for the evening.

The day of your baby shower arrives, you are excited for the day's events. Right on time at 9.00am Hannah, Trevor and baby Nate arrive with all the supplies for the party.

You join Hannah in the kitchen and start to unpack the bags she has bought, "Hey what are you doing there, you need to rest" barks Hannah.

Jolted by Hannah's voice, you look at her, "Sorry, I was seeing what you have in here, I want to help".

"No, you are on rest, I have this under control, your mum is coming soon and will help".

"Oh, come on, I have been resting for the last four weeks, I need to do something, surely there is something I can do?"

Hannah stops and thinks for a bit, "Ok, you can sit there and make up some sandwiches and place them on the platter".

You follow Hannah's instructions and make the sandwiches while Chad, Hannah and Trevor set up the tables and decorations.

Right on time, guests start arriving, and the baby shower gets underway, you are so excited to see everyone, share in the excitement of the impending arrival of your babies, and forget about the health issues and subsequent restrictions for a few hours.

Everyone has so much fun, and the games are a success, and before you know, it the time has come for people to head off. You thank everyone and say your farewells and look at the wonderful array of gifts that everyone has so generously brought for you and your little ones.

Chad joins you as you peruse the multiple clothing, toys and nursery items. "Wow everyone has been so generous, these are such wonderful gifts" you say.

"Yes, it is so wonderful of everyone, how are you feeling are you ok after such a big day?" Chad asks concerned.

"I am great, a little tired, but I have had such a great day".

Just then Hannah comes over, you turn to her and give her a huge bear hug "Thank you Hannah, this has been a fantastic day, you are amazing to do all this".

"My pleasure love, but I can't take all the credit, Chad had a lot of input to".

You turn to Chad, "Thanks sweetheart, this has been a wonderful day".

"My pleasure sweetheart, so glad you enjoyed it."

CHAPTER 27

The last four weeks of your pregnancy begin, and you have been on imposed rest for the last six weeks, and you are eagerly awaiting the birth of your twins. You have supervised Chad as he has finalised the setting up of the nursery, and everything is in place.

You and Chad get ready for your weekly doctor's appointment and this time an ultrasound. As you arrive at the clinic you bump into Derrick and Bree

"Hey, Derrick and Bree, how are you both going?"

"Hey Angela and Chad, great to see you both, we are doing great, we have just had a 20-week scan, we just found out we are having a little girl and she is doing fantastically" replies Derrick, with a smile from ear to ear,

"That is great news guys, I am so happy for you both" you reply, pulling Derrick and Bree in for a hug.

"Thanks Angela, we are so excited, How are you going? the big day is coming soon isn't it?" asks Bree.

"Yes, the official due date is four weeks away, I am doing ok, glad when it is over, and they are here finally".

"I can imagine, Derrick told me about what happened when you collapsed at work, so glad you are ok".

"Thanks Bree, yes it was quite scary, but luckily everything is going well now" you respond.

Just then the nurse calls your name. "Oh, that's us, we better go, great to see you, take care" you say as you and Chad head to the consulting room.

Inside the doctor arrives "Good morning, Angela and Chad, how are we all doing today" the doctor asks smiling.

"We are good, I have been doing as you have instructed, and feel good, anxious for these little ones to arrive though" you say rubbing your belly.

"Well, it shouldn't be too long to go now, as you know, multiples may come earlier than single babies, now let's check your vitals and then we can have a peak at these babies".

After checking your vitals, she advises that everything is in the normal ranges, the doctor starts to prepare for the ultrasound. Suddenly the image of your two babies appears on the screen, the doctor takes some measurements and turns to you both "Well everything is looking as it should be, the babies are growing wonderfully, as I suspected, they are beginning to move into position to prepare for birth, so I don't think it will be too long before they make their appearance".

"Oh really, that is exciting" Chad says as he squeezes your hand.

"Now, are you sure you didn't want to know the genders of the babies?" the doctor asks.

You and Chad look at each other, and reply together, "No, we want it to be a surprise".

"Ok then, well don't look to closely, because the genders are quite obvious in this shot" the doctor laughs.

You and Chad look away from the screen smiling.

The doctor performs some more measurements and observations and then clears you to leave, handing you your ultrasound pictures. "I have chosen pictures that will keep the genders a surprise for you, now I will see you next week, as always call me if anything changes or you have any questions".

"Thanks Doctor" you reply as you get dressed and get ready to leave.

As you head home, you and Chad discuss how relieved you are that everything is fine with the babies. Chad looks at you and asks, "Are you disappointed, we didn't find out the genders today?"

You pause for a moment before answering "No, not really, I want it to be a surprise, besides the doctor said it shouldn't be too long now, How about you? Did you want to find out?"

"Part of me wants to know now, but the other part is happy to wait, as you say not long to go now".

The next few days pass by quickly, winter is finished, and you notice spring is finally on its way, blossoms are forming on the trees, and the sun is shining longer and stronger each day.

As you and Chad enjoy the sun while sitting in the garden, you begin to feel some discomfort in your belly, but you decide not to mention it to Chad and dismiss it as it passes quickly, and you put it down to the babies moving around.

As the day progresses, the discomfort continues, and by early evening, the discomfort is getting stronger, and Chad notices your reaction "Is everything ok? Are you alright" he asks concerned.

You reply, "Yes, I am fine, just a little stomach cramp is all,"

"Really how long has this been going on" asks Chad.

"Oh, since late morning, but it's nothing, it passes quickly".

Chad cuts you off panicking "What? Why didn't you say something sooner, do you think we need to go to the hospital?"

"No, No, it's nothing, it's fine, remember from our birthing classes, contractions are usually more intense and closer together, relax it's fine".

"Ok, I wish you had told me earlier, tell me if it gets any worse Ok" Chad responds, and you can sense his growing concern.

"Of course, sweetheart, now let's relax and enjoy the DVD you have picked out."

Chad continues to watch you like a hawk for the rest of the evening, not leaving your side. As you both prepare for bed, Chad looks at you and asks again, "How are you feeling, has anything changed?"

"No darling, still just a little discomfort at times, nothing intense, don't worry, let's just go to sleep".

"Ok, but you wake me if the feelings get any worse alright?" Chad says seriously as he waves his finger at you for extra emphasis.

"Don't worry you will know if it gets worse," you laugh as you get into bed. Chad snuggles up behind you, encapsulating you in his protective embrace and you both fall asleep.

After only a few hours, Chad jolts you awake quickly. "Sweetheart wake up, quick, I think your waters are breaking".

You wake up to a sharp pain in your belly and notice that your waters have broken "Oh no, ouch, it is really hurting now, sorry about the bed".

Chad is frantically dressing and says, "Don't worry about that, let's get to the hospital now, are you ok?,"

"Yes, oh wow, here comes another pain" you cry out as you grab Chad's hand squeezing it hard.

Once the pain subsides, Chad helps you to the car and rushes you to the hospital.

As you arrive at the hospital, the nurses help you and Chad to a birthing suite and settles you in, reassuring you.

Shortly after your doctor arrives.

"Hello, guys, looks like things are happening now, let's have a look and see how you are progressing".

The doctor examines you, and then advises that you are close to halfway to being fully dilated and that things could still be a little while off, she prescribes an epidural for you.

Chad takes your hands, "Oh my goodness, we are going to meet our babies soon".

"Yes, looks like it" you reply just as another sharp contraction hits.

Hours pass, the epidural has taken effect and the doctor arrives to examine you, She checks your chart, decides to take your blood pressure herself, looking at the result, she looks at you and asks "Angela, how are you feeling right now?"

"I am ok, a bit nervous and excited".

"Do you have a headache at all?"

"Well maybe a little bit,"

"Are you feeling any nausea? or blurred vision?"

"Well, a little bit, but I thought that it was normal for labour, why is there something wrong" you ask.

The doctor looks at you both "Your blood pressure is getting a little bit higher than I would like, and with your past preeclampsia, I am feeling that we may need to do a c- section to deliver these babies".

"Oh really, is that necessary?"

"Well, I will just keep an eye on things right now, if your readings get any higher, we will do an emergency caesarean, but it is ok to proceed as is for the moment. I will get the nurses to check your vitals every 30 minutes and keep me updated and I will come back in the next hour to see how things are progressing, just try to relax as much as possible ok"

"Easier said than done doctor".

Several hours pass, and the doctor returns, "Hey Angela, things are progressing well, I am happy to report that your blood pressure seems to be holding steady, so we feel confident that we can progress with a natural birth," the doctor says with a reassuring smile.

"Oh, that is a relief, how much longer do you think it will be before the babies are actually born" you ask with a tired smile.

"Let me examine you and see how things are looking", she replies, "Ok, very good, we are almost there, I would estimate any time within the next hour or so."

"Oh well that will be soon" replies Chad as he squeezes your hand, with excitement.

"Great, I will be just outside nearby, and the nurses will keep an eye on you all and will notify me if anything changes, just try to relax, it should not be too much longer" says the doctor as she heads out the door.

Chad turns to you, "Sweetheart, that is great news, our babies are nearly here, Hannah, Trev and our parents are all outside, I will just pop out to update them and be right back" he leans down and kisses you on the forehead before leaving you with a nurse who is still busy updating your notes with the latest observations and doctor's comments.

"Angela, you are doing great, this is an exciting time for you and Chad" the nurse says with a smile.

"Thanks, I am excited, anxious and scared all at the same time".

"Don't worry, we are all here with you".

A little while later, Chad returns, "I just updated everyone, there is quite a crowd forming out there, they are all so excited."

"Oh, that is great, hopefully it won't be too much longer then".

A little while later, the nurse comes over and looks at the printout of the baby heart rate monitor next to you. As you watch her, you see her face change to one of concern, you ask worriedly "What's wrong, is everything ok?"

"The monitor is showing that one of the babies' heart rate is a little more elevated, I will just go an update the doctor" and she quickly leaves the room.

You turn to Chad, stretching out your hand, "Oh no, what if something is wrong" you say as tears form in your eyes.

Chad is equally concerned, but tries to remain strong for you, he squeezes your hand, "let us just see what the doctor says".

You both anxiously wait for the doctor to return and examine the printout. After discussions with the nurse, she turns to both you and Chad, "Ok, yes, one of the babies appears to be suffering a little bit of stress, but nothing too serious at this stage, as the birth is very close now, we don't foresee any problems, but we will keep a close eye on the monitor here, I will stay with you now as looking at the other observations, your babies will be coming very soon."

You and Chad look at each with a mixture of relief, excitement and anxiety. You are both about to see your new babies for the first time.

The nursing staff prepare you for the birth, and shortly after the doctor encourages you to push, squeezing Chad's hand tightly you push with all your might and your first baby is born.

"Congratulations, you have a beautiful little girl" the doctor says as she hands your newly born daughter to waiting nursing staff to be cleaned up and checked.

"Now Angela, you can have a little break, but it is not over yet, your second baby will be arriving any minute now. Are you nearly ready to go again?" the doctor says.

"Well, no, but I don't really have a choice do I" you respond with a little chuckle.

"Good, you still have your sense of humour Angela" replies the doctor with a smile.

Chad holds your hand tightly, encouraging you, but also keeping an eye on his new baby girl with the nursing staff.

"Come on sweetheart, you got this, just a little bit further to go, and it will be all over, and we will have two little munchkins, I am so proud of you sweetheart".

Just then, the doctor tells you to push again and before you know it, your second baby is born. You lay back on the bed, crying with relief that you have made it.

"Congratulations, you have a beautiful little boy, you have done a fantastic job Angela" the doctor says.

"Oh sweetheart, you did it, we have two beautiful babies, a girl and a boy." Says Chad with tears in his eyes as he leans down to kiss you.

"Are they ok?" you ask.

"We will just do a quick couple of checks, your son was the one that was showing signs of distress on the monitor. and we will bring them over to you in a second, just relax, the hard part is done now, great job" replies the doctor.

"Oh no, will he be ok?" Chad asks with concern.

Minutes later, they nurses bring your new babies over to you and place them on your chest.

The doctor joins you, "I have checked them both, and they are fine, I will let you both have a quick hold, they need to have a little bit of oxygen after the birth."

You and Chad can't hold back your tears as you both look at your babies.

Shortly after you reluctantly return the babies back to the nurses so they can receive the oxygen and post birth care they require. The nurse moves you back to your room, where you can freshen up a little. The nurses later come in with your babies.

"Hello, we have two little bundles here that want to see their Mummy and Daddy" says one nurse as she wheels in the crib carrying your new daughter, closely followed by another nurse with your new son.

Chad rushes to the cribs, and wheels them to the bed next to you. "Hello sweeties we missed you" he says softly to the two little ones. "Are they Ok now?", he asks the nurses.

"Yes, the doctor has given them the all clear, they are a very strong healthy pair of beauties, they can't wait to see their Mummy and Daddy." the nurses smile excitedly.

Chad picks up his daughter and holds her tight kissing her gently on the head and then hands her to you, before reaching down to his son,

"Congratulations you two, they are perfect little angels," says one nurse.

The other asks "Do we have names for these two yet?"

You and Chad turn to each other smiling, you respond "Yes we do actually" looking down at your new baby daughter, you continue. "Yes, this is Lexie".

And then Chad speaks, "And this is Evan".

"Oh, they are gorgeous names," says the nurses as they head to leave the room "We will leave you all now to bond together, Oh by the way Chad, congratulations, it is Father's day today, what a fantastic present".

Chad turns to you, "Oh my goodness, it is Father's day today, I didn't realise, how awesome is that, Thank you sweetheart, I am so happy."

You respond with a laugh, "I can't take the credit for that darling, these two wanted to surprise you for your first Father's day."

You both watch your babies resting peacefully in your arms.

You look at Chad and smile "Well sweetheart, Lexie and Evan are finally here, it was little later than we had originally scheduled, but our family is now complete".

Chad kisses you and replies "Yes sweetheart, our family is now complete".